THE CAMP

By
Greg Hair

Text copyright © 2013 Greg Hair
All rights reserved.

ISBN-13: 9781479356676
ISBN-10: 1479356670
Library of Congress Control Number: 2013916032
CreateSpace Independent Publishing Platform
North Charleston, South Carolina

This book is dedicated to all the nameless faces of children and adults that I encountered, in photographs and film footage, during my research. Some survived; most didn't.

CHAPTER ONE

1993

"I hate being Jewish," said the young, dark-haired boy, walking into Louisville's Jewish Community Center. He threw his blue backpack against the white brick interior of the lobby, and slid down the wall to the floor. He was already beginning to sweat from the small walk he made from the school bus to the building.

"Now, Benjamin, why do you say that?" asked an old man in a thick German accent, coming around from behind the welcome desk. He brought with him a basket of fresh bagels, sitting it on a table near the entrance. His white hair formed a cow lick, like an ocean wave crashing against a rocky shoal. "It's a hot day out there. This was the last day of school, wasn't it?"

Benjamin nodded, and the old man noticed that the aroma of the fresh baked bread drew the boy's attention.

"Would you like a bottle of water?"

Benjamin again nodded.

The old man went behind his desk, and returned seconds later with a bottled water in hand. "Now, I'm sorry, Benjamin, tell me why it is you hate being Jewish."

"You can call me, Benji, Mister Engel."

"But, of course, Benji," said the old man, smiling.

"A friend at school, Mister Engel. He called me Judenscheisse." Benji paused, looking as if he were waiting for a certain facial expression from Mister Engel, like he had said something he shouldn't have. "I think I said that right. I don't know what that means; I don't even know what language it is."

"It's German. Your friend speaks German?" Mister Engel pulled a still-hot bagel from the basket, and handed it to the boy.

"His grandfather does. He told him that word." Benji drank half the bottle of water before he withdrew it from his lips.

"Well, Jewshit is what it means," the old man whispered, seeing several women approach the building's entrance, "and it doesn't sound like he's much of a friend if he's making you wish you weren't Jewish. I promise you that he knew what the word meant when he used it."

Mister Engel, seeing the look of astonishment on Benji's face at what the old man just said, turned his attention to the women as they entered, checking their membership passes, though he knew who they were, and passing them a clipboard so they could sign in.

"What's wrong with the boy?" asked one of the women.

"Oh, just some trouble at school," he said. "You know how kids are."

"You're so good with the children, Mister Engel," she said, grabbing a bagel. The woman turned to her friends as they walked away. "He's a volunteer, here. He's so good with the children."

"He used to be my friend," Benji continued, watching the women turn a corner, "but says he doesn't want to anymore because I'm Jewish. He said his dad, and grandfather, don't like Jews, so he doesn't, either. You speak German?"

"A little." The old man struggled to reach the floor, next to the eight-year-old boy, without requiring the calling of an ambulance. "Your friend's dad has certain beliefs and has now passed them on to his son."

The boy turned his head away from the old man's sight, sniffed, and wiped his cheek with his hand.

"You thought this other boy was a friend, but he turned out to be the opposite," Mister Engel said, looking out the glass entrance to see two dark-suited men approaching the doors. "You're in elementary school, right?"

Benji nodded. "I go to fifth grade next year."

"I'd say that you learned a valuable lesson today, son. You are learning to expect the unexpected from people. Never let your guard down—for you know not who it is that sits next to you."

"What, Mister Engel?"

The old man looked back down at the boy, who starred back up at him, obviously having no clue what the man was talking about.

The Camp

"You never truly know what is in someone's heart," the old man said, with grave intent.

The front doors swung open as the two men entered.

"Excuse me, we were told a Karl Engel worked here, at the front desk," said the older, more distinguished looking man, with thick blond hair. His partner, a much younger man with brown hair, stood behind him.

"I am Karl Engel," the old man said. "May I help you?"

"I'm Agent Williams," said the lead man, showing his Federal Bureau of Investigation identification. "This is Agent Stein. You need to come with us, sir."

"What's going on, Mister Engel?" asked Benji. "Who are they?"

"It's okay," Mister Engel said. "It's just some business that needs to be taken care of…finally."

"I would prefer not to do this in front of the child. Please, stand and come with us."

"I am a tired, old man, and I know why you're here. If you came looking for me in a public place, you can take the next step publicly."

"Very well," the man sighed, nodding to his cohort who immediately grabbed Mister Engel's arms and helped him, somewhat roughly, to his feet. "You are under arrest for crimes against humanity for your work as a guard in one of Nazi-occupied Poland's concentration and extermination camps. I'm now going to read to you your Miranda rights."

"Don't bother. I know my rights and I waive them all. I have no need for an attorney."

"Sir, please. I must read you your rights, after that, you may do as you wish, though I highly recommend you retain an attorney."

Mister Engel, being handcuffed, turned to Benji. "You need to run along, now. It's time for you to go down to where the other kids are. Tell one of the workers that someone needs to come watch the front desk."

Benji left his water, bagel, and backpack sitting on the floor, taking off down the hall.

Following the reading of Karl Engel's Miranda rights, the old man was led out of the Jewish Community Center and to a waiting black sedan.

Sitting in the backseat, on polished brown leather, next to the younger agent, Karl noticed that sometime during the journey to the car, the officer had pulled his necklace, upon which a gold Star of David hung, out from underneath his shirt. The smell of Brute aftershave permeated the car's interior.

"Does this bother you?" asked the young officer, rubbing the star between his thumb and forefinger. "Like a cross for vampires?"

"I will tell you everything you want to know," said Karl, "but I want my son present when I do."

"Does your son not know about you?" asked Williams.

"No. He knows nothing."

"Are you sure you want him there? You sure you want him to know everything? I'm willing to bring him in if it means getting a confession, but are you sure you want him there at this time? Wouldn't it be best for you to speak with him in private once we've finished?"

"I'll confess to what I've done. And yes, I want him there. Also, I would like to see my wife."

"Sorry," Williams said, from the driver's seat. "That's not going to happen. I'll arrange for your son, but we have to take you immediately to the local FBI office downtown to be processed. Besides, I know that you don't have a wife, at least, not anymore. I don't mean to sound cruel, sir, but we have a file on you back at the office, and it says your wife is deceased."

"You have a file?" Karl stared out the window. "How long have you been looking for me?"

"Not long, actually. When our intelligence received the tip a couple of days ago, we contacted The Simon Wiesenthal Center who told us something interesting—the Nazi known as Karl Engel was killed in World War Two."

"Seems to me that your intelligence isn't all that intelligent. You called the New York office of the Wiesenthal organization, didn't you?"

"Yeah," said Stein. "So?"

"So, I suspect you'll be getting a call from a different office soon."

"Well," Williams began, "the person who identified you in the first place is extremely confident, nonetheless, of your identity. So, as you can understand, we're quite interested in you. Knowing your age, however, and knowing that you were unaware that we were looking into you, we knew you weren't going anywhere."

"Yet, it took two of you to arrest an old man. As far as my wife having passed, that's true, but that doesn't mean I can't see her. See her grave, I mean."

The Camp

"Yeah, sure," said the young Jewish officer. "You'd love for us to just take you there, like we don't have orders to follow. You know better than that. You know what it's like to have to follow orders. Isn't that what all you guys say? You were just following orders?"

"You know nothing," said Karl. "No self-respecting Nazi would ever say he was just following orders. He did what he did not just because he was told to, but because he wanted to."

"David," began the senior officer, "I mean, Agent Stein, be careful. Don't cross the line. He still has rights."

Several minutes linger in silence, as the car continues toward downtown Louisville, the East End of Jefferson County moving swiftly by, when David leans into Karl's car.

"So, what were you talking to that kid about back there when we picked you up?"

Quiet seconds passed.

"I bet you like to watch the kids, don't you?" David continued whispering. "You probably imagine them in their little striped outfits, right? The ones the prisoners had to wear in the camps. I wonder, what would you do to that kid, the one you were talking to when you were finally caught, if you had the chance?"

Karl turned his head toward David, staring coldly into his eyes. "Children his age would not have made it to the striped outfits."

"You son-of-a-bitch, I think you actually *want* to tell me what you would do," said Agent Stein. "Yours is an interesting case. A Nazi actually hiding among Jews; the wolf mixing with the sheep. I've never heard that one before. It's clever. I mean, we found you actually still keeping an eye on Jews." He leaned back to his side of the backseat, away from Mister Engel. "Well, it *was* clever, until someone recognized you."

Mister Engel's eyes squinted.

"That's enough, officer," said the senior man, turning the car into the parking garage of the FBI's Louisville field office. "We're here."

Karl faced forward again, saying nothing.

CHAPTER TWO

"Would you like a cup of coffee, Mister Engel?" asked Agent Williams, removing his black jacket, throwing it on the back of a green leather chair. He set his file on the silver, metallic table that occupied the middle of the room. "Maybe a water, instead? It's very hot outside. I feel like I'm covered in sweat just from walking from the parking garage. We've contacted your son, and he's on his way."

The white room already had a strong coffee odor, and Karl wondered how many cups, during all the interrogations that had taken place, had been drunk in there. He noticed the ubiquitous mirror on the far side of the room, and wondered if there was already someone standing on the opposite side, watching him.

"You're not really going to offer him something are you?" asked Agent Stein.

"Water would be fine," said Karl Engel.

"Agent Stein, please step out into the hall, and take a few moments to yourself. You may come back in when you feel you can handle it. Like it or not, he's still an American citizen."

The young officer stared at his senior partner, turned toward Karl, then huffed and left the room.

"Sorry about that," said Williams. "Someone thought this interrogation would be good as his first. I disagreed, given the nature of it, but I was overruled."

"The boy is emotionally invested," Karl said, sitting, unrestrained, in his green chair.

A sudden knock from outside the interrogation room interrupted the conversation. Agent Williams opened the door, letting in a man around fifty years of age, escorted by another agent.

"Mister Engel's son, Aaron, I presume?"

"Yes. Dad, what's this all about?" Karl's son quickly shook Williams' hand, and hurried over to his father. The younger Engel loosened his red tie that hung in front of his white shirt.

Before Karl could answer, an old woman entered the room, ushered by Agent Stein, looking calmer than when he left. Aaron Engel stood to the side, watching the scene play out.

"Ma'am, I'm Agent Williams," said the lead man, extending his hand to hers, helping the woman across the room, "and I'm terribly sorry to have to ask you this question, but is this the man who killed your husband? Is this the man you identified at the Jewish Community Center?"

The old woman shuffled across the white floor of the white room, her slightly hunched back seeming to still the carry the burden of something long since passed.

Karl looked into her eyes, searching for recognition, knowing she was doing the same with him. Just as her body belied an unfathomable weight, her eyes betrayed the witnessing of a dark event that had brought both of them to this white room, of someone who had seen brutal death first hand.

"Is your name Karl?" she asked in a strong Eastern European accent, her bottom lip quivering.

"I carry the name Karl with great pride, yes."

"Have you ever worn a Nazi uniform?"

"I have."

Her hand suddenly sped across his face, slapping him, leaving a red print on his left cheek.

"I would recognize your cold, blue, lifeless eyes anywhere," she said. She turned to Agent Williams. "This is him. This is the man who killed my husband in nineteen forty-three."

"Now, wait just a damn minute," said Aaron.

"Thank you, ma'am," said Williams. "That will be all." He opened the door to escort her out.

"Wait," said Karl, suddenly. "I would like for her to stay." Karl turned to his son. "Your mother and I, me especially, always feared, yet knew, this day would come. Thankfully, she passed before it came to fruition. But, the day is here, nonetheless, and it is time you knew the truth about me. I would like for everyone in this room, right now, to remain and listen. It's time for this enormous weight to be lifted."

"Mister Engel," began Williams, "you can't really expect for this woman to listen to you speak about what you did to her husband. Hasn't she dealt with it enough over the years without hearing the details from the murderer, himself?"

"She must stay. I would also like to have Agent Stein present. Yes, all those who have been involved, up until now, must be in this room. Those are my conditions."

"I am not about to have her relive—."

The old woman turned her worn body toward Karl. "I will stay. I was there when it happened, and survived his brutality. There is no more he can do to me."

"Okay. Stein, please get our guest some water. We also need the recorder, and a couple of extra chairs." Agent Stein quickly left the room, the door slowly shutting behind him.

"Pop," said Aaron, "you don't have to do this. They obviously have the wrong guy. We need to get a lawyer, get you out of here, and sue."

"No, son. I have run for too long."

"You haven't run from anything, you never have." Aaron looked at Agent Williams. "This woman obviously has made a mistake. You're going on a memory that's fifty years old. Clearly she's made a mistake." He turned to the old woman. "Ma'am, I'm very sorry for what happened to your husband, and I don't know why my father is admitting to something like this, but this can't continue."

"Sir," said Williams, "I tried to get your father to retain a lawyer, but he refused. I tried to get him to speak to you in private about all of this, after we finished our business, but he again, refused. Now, we are in contact with both Poland, and Germany, though we're not sure which country will extradite."

"Extradite?" asked Aaron. "There's not going to be an extradition. He didn't do anything."

"Sir, how much do you know about your father?"

"Everything."

"Nothing," said Karl Engel. "You really know nothing about me, which means that I've also hidden a large part of who you are. I'm sorry, son. I should have told you the truth a long time ago."

Agent Stein entered the room, a chair in each hand, a tape recorder under one arm, and a bottle of water under the other. He shut the door behind him. Everyone took a seat.

"Okay, Mister Engel," Williams said. "We're all here." He pressed the record button.

"Before I begin," said Karl, "you must know that I do not deny that I have killed, nor do I deny that I have worn the uniform of the SS, and for that, I am willing to stand trial. However, you will not be charging me with war crimes, or crimes against humanity, or anything else of that nature."

"And, just why is that?" asked Agent Stein. "You just admitted to what you're accused of."

"Because, in nineteen forty-three, a man's life was saved, a man named Albert Fogel."

"Albert Fogel? Who the hell is that? If you think you can get away with committing crimes against humanity, because one man was saved, you're wrong."

"Your response, and ignorance, is exactly why you need to be here, to listen to what I have to say."

"Please, Mister Engel," said Williams, "begin your story."

Karl Engel looked around the room, making sure he had everyone's attention. The cool air from the vent above blew across his white hair. His son sat in a chair in a corner, looking at him, shaking his head.

"Don't do it, pop."

"Son, listen closely," said Karl, his heart pounding as he began to speak of long-passed events for the first time in fifty years. "I was eighteen-years-old when my life changed forever…"

CHAPTER THREE

February, 1943

Karl Engel stood alone as the train pulled into the unloading area of the camp and hushed out its remaining steam. Watching the smoke from the fires of the nearest crematorium rise to meet the flaming colors of the setting sun, he felt the biting, cold, winter wind run through his crisp gray Nazi uniform and wrap itself around his bones. He didn't feel as cold as he should have, though; a few glasses of Jagermeister saw to that. He also knew he wasn't nearly as cold as the incoming cargo.

"Hey, Karl!"

The young guard turned to see three laughing comrades huddled together, standing around a fire built inside an old oil drum.

"You should have had more to drink, Karl," said Klaus, one of the other guards. "There are a few more Guterwagens attached to this train. More coming in means we'll be outside longer."

"What?" asked Wilhelm, another guard. "Karl drink more? He drinks like a woman as it is. I bet Leni Riefenstahl could outdrink him."

"Yeah, only a woman could drink more than a woman," said Hans.

Karl smiled as the other three broke out in laughter. Of all four guards, only Klaus had the 'pure' German look, the blond hair and blue eyes that pervaded the language spoken by the hierarchy of the Nazi party when referring to the highest ideal of human genetics. His height, at just under six feet, and broad shoulders, also leant an air of superiority that he generally employed when dealing with other guards.

Leadership of the group of four often split between Karl and Klaus, more of a power-share than a struggle, both men having mutual respect for the other, while Hans and Wilhelm typified the followers that all leaders must have. The latter two shared much of the same physical attributes as Karl, dark hair and eyes, though a little shorter, coming in at around five-and-a-half feet, and falling somewhat lower on the intelligence scale in comparison to their friends.

Moments later, SS doctors, all dressed in white, emerged from the buildings behind Karl with their tables and papers. A white van with a red cross painted on its side sat parked nearby—part of the ruse to keep the new arrivals calm.

"Looks like it's going to be a beautiful night," said the doctor assigned to Karl's train car. "Not a cloud in the sky."

A vinyl album of Richard Wagner's music crackled and popped from the speakers overhead.

Karl stepped forward to the nearest train car, unlatched the lock, and slid the car's door back.

"Out Jews!" he yelled. "Out! Get out!"

The other guards joined the operation, positioning themselves at various cars to unload their cargo onto the ramp.

"Men in one line; women and children in another!" Karl continued. "Come Jews, hurry! The faster you move, the sooner you will fill your bellies! Do not worry about the dead on the train—they are no longer worried about you!"

A multitude of men, women, and children were ushered out of their respective transports and into the bitter, cold, darkening night air. They huddled together, as best they could, while trying to stay in single-file lines.

Karl walked up and down the platform, checking the armbands worn by the new arrivals in the bright electrical lights. The yellow triangles being overlaid by inverted ones of various colors, to form the Star of David, told him right away to which direction certain Jews would be immediately sent. Some had an added 'P' in the middle of their star, informing him that there were some Polish Jews mixed with the German ones.

The arrivals watched him as he passed, especially the children, snuggled against their mothers, their little hands wrapped in the large coats of their maternal guardians. Karl did the best he could not to make eye contact with the young ones, trying to keep his gaze level with the adults, though his eyes wandered now and then toward the ground.

The Camp

And they would stare right back, their eyes locked onto his, as if waiting for the next command. He also noticed that, when he did look down, the large hands would pull the children close. Big or small, young or old, all of the new arrivals had a putrid, urine smell after being so tightly packed in a train car for days. Karl imagined it was much worse in the summertime.

One crying baby, in the latter half of the line, caught his attention.

"Madam, please quiet your baby," he said. The infant's wails hammered Karl's already ringing ears, the alcohol in his system affecting his already shortened fuse. He ran his hand across his forehead.

"Karl," began the doctor nearest the young man, "I'm afraid I've left my pen inside. Please begin the selection process while I retrieve it." The pudgy man, with his eyeglasses perched on the tip of his nose, started up the steps to the warmth inside.

"Yes, sir."

Karl pulled his jacket down and straightened his posture, preparing his diaphragm for a long vocal reach. He watched everyone shake, unsure whether it was the cold, or fear, or both, that caused their miniature convulsions. The mothers with babies did their best to keep them quiet, and warm, holding them as close to their coats as they could without smothering them. Though, there was the one that continued to cry the loudest.

"I've already told you," Karl yelled down the line, "to get that baby quiet!"

All the new arrivals ahead of that particular baby, turned to look, trying to see which one wasn't cooperating. The infant's cries became muffled as those adults around the mother began sounding like the hushed steam released from the stopped train.

"Now, attention, Jews!" he continued, "Attention! Face forward! It is freezing, and I do not want to be out here any longer than I have to! I will tell each of you to move either to the left, or the right. Listen well, and move quickly in your assigned direction. You will then proceed to your hot showers, leaving your luggage where it is now. It will be returned to you later."

Karl began moving down the path that lay between the two lines, moving his head from side to side as he called out, inspecting each Jew he saw.

"Left. Left," he began, sending the first two men, both elderly gentlemen, to a smiling, waiting guard who waved the men to the next checkpoint.

"Right," he said to another, more youthful male. He continued along, criss-crossing the path that lay before him, directing each person to one of the two guards standing behind him.

"Right," he said, to the next woman in the parallel line. She leaned back as he got closer, her face distorted, as she began walking toward the guard on the right.

"Stop," said Karl. "What's the matter? Does the smell of real German liquor bother you? It's nothing compared to that Jew smell of yours. And that doesn't include all the Jew piss that covers you. As a matter of fact, I think I just changed my mind about where to send you." He smiled. "Left!"

The Nazi guard on the left suddenly grabbed the woman, jerking her from her previous destination on the right, yelling at her to follow the others on the left.

"Right," he said to the next man in line, an older gentleman, who, Karl noticed, stared at him with intense eyes. As the man moved along, Karl looked back and saw the man still looking at him.

"What are you looking at, Jew?" Karl asked. "Eyes forward."

"He knows a beautiful woman when he sees one," said Hans, one of Karl's guard friends. "Heh, Leni?"

Laughter ensued among the various guards within earshot.

Karl, still making eye-contact with the older man, reached for the Walther P38 that hung at his side.

"Wait!" said the doctor, returning to his table. "Karl, what are you doing? This man has radial dysplasia."

Karl gave the doctor a dumbfounded look.

"He has clubhand," the doctor responded. "He cannot work. He must go to the left."

"My apologies, Herr Doctor." Karl watched as the man, whose gaze continued to meet his own, moved from one guard, to the other, in the direction of the rising smoke, and out of sight. "I should have sent him in that direction in the first place, clubhand, or not, the way he was eyeballing me."

"Quite alright, Karl. But, you must pay better attention next time. We want able workers. Remember—right means 'right to work.' I'll take over from here."

"Daddy?" Karl heard, snapping his head around toward the end of the line to see a young girl sticking her head out, watching the man with the clubhand disappear. An older woman pulled the girl back in.

The Camp

Karl moved back to the head of the two lines as the doctor continued the sorting process, taking only seconds to decide which direction to send each man, woman, and child.

"It is too cold out here for me, and this is taking too long," said the doctor. "All Jew women, listen! If you have young children, please step out of line and proceed to the guard on the left!"

Wagner's music continued throughout the process.

Karl noticed the mother who previously held the crying baby, stepped out and moved to the left. The baby no longer cried. He stopped her, and opened the shawl wrapped around her child—the now dead infant.

"What did you do?" he asked, looking at her in horror.

"I tried to keep him quiet for you," she said, still rocking the body. "I was afraid of what you would do to him."

"Herr Engel," began the doctor, "does it really matter what she did to her baby? She's going to the left, anyway."

Karl wrapped the baby back up as the doctor waved the mother on.

"Please, doctor," began the next-to-last woman in line, trying to speak through the sound of shuffling feet heading to the left, her arm wrapped around the young girl who had called out for her father. "Where did that man go? The one with the clubhand?"

"No talking, Jew!" said Karl. He noticed the young girl's brown eyes staring at him, almost with the same intensity as the older man.

"It's alright," the doctor said, smiling warmly.

The man in white scanned the woman up and down, then looked at the waif-of-a-girl next to her.

"Why, he went to be fed, madam. You will receive your meal after going to the right. How old are you, and how old is this girl?"

"I am forty-years-old," said the woman. "She is fourteen." Karl watched the woman's arm tighten around the child, both shivering. "But, you said he could not work. What does that mean?"

"I assure you, we find a purpose for each Jew that comes here. Is she your daughter?"

"Yes."

"The man was your husband?"

"Yes."

"Don't worry, he is being taken to a warm place. Just like you. The girl is a little scrawny. Did you two not eat well enough in your ghetto?"

The guards near him laughed.

"We were appreciative of what we had," she said.

"Mmm-hmm. To the right, both of you. Next."

The last woman, a young woman, looking to be in her late-teens, with wavy, shoulder-length, brown hair, and large brown eyes, stepped forward.

Karl looked her over a couple of times then looked away, displaying disgust, when her eyes met his.

"And, your age?" asked the doctor.

"I'm sixteen."

The doctor, like Karl, examined her as well, his eyes moving slowly over her body. "Too bad you're a Jew. One could have called you pretty. Go to the right."

Having completed the processing of new arrivals, the doctor looked at Karl, who stood next to the warm steam still hissing out from under the train.

"Please help escort these women to the barber, then their showers," said the pudgy doctor.

Karl followed along, trailing the last three women, as the larger group followed two guards ahead of them.

"Where did daddy go?" Karl heard the young girl whisper to her mother. The woman turned and looked at him.

"Quiet," he said. "No talking. There will be time to talk later."

Ushering the tail-end of the human train into the barber, where other prisoners awaited to remove the hair of new arrivals, Karl continued to keep a close, clandestine eye on the sixteen-year-old brunette from outside. Anytime she caught him looking, he gave the same look of repulsion as he had back at the train.

He chuckled, from time to time, as multiple women cried, watching their hair fall, sometimes in clumps, other times like feathers, to the floor, each woman now beginning to look identical to the others with their nearly bald scalps.

Like shearing sheep, he thought, thinking back to childhood days spent on his grandfather's farm.

The Camp

Quickly, Karl and the other guards moved them out and onto the next stage of processing—picking up their striped pajamas, with most of the new outfits being one or two sizes too big.

Finally, reaching a small, concrete room, in the basement of a building, the women huddled together as one of the guards stood on a box and called their attention.

"What I am about to say is also being heard by those who were told to go to the left during processing only a few moments ago. Theirs, however, will have a slight variation." A low chuckle arose from the guards. "Now, if you would, please begin undressing, as I speak. In the next room, you will be given a shower and, after such, your meal. You are now in a labor camp and if you wish to be free, remember this—work makes you free. You will each be assigned a place to sleep, which is run by a Kapo, one of your own that will oversee your work. Once everyone is ready, you will all be moved into the shower room. Thank you for your cooperation."

"Though no amount of showering can get rid of that Jew smell you pointed out, right?" said Wilhelm, a smiling guard standing next to Karl.

Karl didn't answer as Klaus, another guard, walked over.

"Karl, you in this time?" he asked.

"Yes. After the showers," said Karl, pushing the group of nude women from behind, corralling them into the shower room.

He heard the desperate whispering, the palpable anxiety, rising among the women. The majority cried.

Once the last female had entered, the guards closed the steel doors, locking them. Karl listened, emotionless, to the screams of the fearful women inside.

CHAPTER FOUR

Once the group shower had finished, Karl and the three other guards ushered the majority of the nude women out of the basement and into the outside cold, the women already trembling from the freezing water that had poured over them, while ordering a few to remain behind.

The shower room smelled of urine, the warm liquid released by fear when all the women thought they were about to die. The yellow puddles on the gray concrete floor had been diluted with cold water that had rained from the shower heads that hung from above, each head about ten feet from another, connected to a line of exposed piping. The bodily fluids had been diluted, but the odor remained.

The room spun as Karl closed his eyes, his head soaked in alcohol. Feeling his dizziness encapsulate him, he opened his eyes, struggling to keep them that way. All he wanted to do was pass out. Putting one hand on a wall to steady himself, he ran the other over his eyes.

"Which one do you want, Karl?" asked Hans.

Karl looked at the other three guards, who were promptly undressing, then at the four already nude women standing in a far corner of the shower room, huddled together, their arms intertwined, forming what looked like one grotesque, four-headed, multi-limbed creature. He focused his increasingly blurred vision on one face in particular—the brunette from the train.

She stood several inches shorter than his five-foot, eleven-inch stature, with big, brown eyes. No matter how hard he tried, no matter how disgusted he was at her Jewishness, he couldn't keep from looking at her, the last woman in the processing line.

The devil can be quite beautiful, he thought. *But, I won't let him, or her, get their claws in me.*

Still trying to focus on the one girl, and realizing he continuously made a mistake when he closed his eyes, fooling his brain into thinking it was time to pass out, he shuffled his feet over to the corner, and grabbed her by the arm. She trembled, but didn't resist.

The other guards quickly made their selections, and each couple took a corner. None of the girls put up a fight.

Karl forced the young woman around, turning her back to him, and bent her over, as he struggled and fumbled unzipping his pants. Her skin felt cold from her shower, goosebumps covering her flesh. He scanned the cranial contours and the few tiny moles on her now visible scalp. Not thinking, trying to grab her by the back of her head, Karl grasped nothing but a handful of loose, wet hair. His eyes rolled in their sockets, his brain wanting desperately to shut down. Her body convulsed as he touched her, and he heard her quiet whimpering, but beyond that, there was no physical reaction. No struggle; no crying out.

Karl's head flopped around, looking at the others, and noticed the same thing—all the women were compliant. One girl began to cry slightly louder than the others, but quickly silenced herself when her guard, Klaus, withdrew his member, picked up his pistol, and placed the black metallic barrel to the back of her head.

Karl fumbled inside his pants with one hand, while rubbing the girl's backside with his other.

"I never thought I'd get to have sex when I volunteered for this job," said Wilhelm.

"Sex?" asked Klaus. "Sex is what you have with women, with real people. When you're fucking animals, it's called bestiality. Didn't you learn anything in school?"

The guards' laughter echoed around the concrete room, reverberating in Karl's inebriated ears.

He stumbled backward, regained his balance, and realized he still didn't have an erection.

"Yours just doesn't do it for you, Karl?" asked Hans, finishing up with his woman. "Would you like mine?"

"Maybe he wants that old man from the train, the one that kept looking at him," said Klaus, extracting himself, and pushing her aside. The girl fell into a puddle of water, urine, and blood, her virginity having become just another possession taken by the Nazis.

"Maybe it's his first time, and he doesn't know what to do. Maybe that Jew's parts aren't in the right place."

"You don't look so good, Karl," said Hans, still in the middle of raping his selection. "You okay?"

Karl shook his head, walked to one of the drains in the cold floor, dropped to his knees, and vomited. He finally collapsed onto his side, rolled over, and came to rest in a small puddle.

Klaus and the other two guards laughed, sauntering over in the nude, toward Karl.

"Now get out, Jews!" yelled Hans. "We need to shower to get this filth off that you got on us. You're so disgusting."

"Witch Jews!" said Klaus. "Vexing us with your evil ways! Turning our bodies against us; forcing yourselves on us!"

The women, blood running down the legs of each of them, except for the young woman who was with Karl, her virginity still intact, moved sheepishly toward the exit, continuously looking back at the guards.

"Go!" screamed Wilhelm. "Get out before we shoot you for what you've done. Just look what you've done to Karl! If you've hurt him, we'll kill all of you!"

The women finally exited the shower room as the three guards bent over Karl, making sure he was okay. Klaus went out the room's entrance, turned on the water, and came back in. Each guard took a different shower head, the three leaving Karl on the floor to take care of himself. After washing themselves, and making sure Karl's vomit went down the drain, Klaus turned the showers off. Hans passed out the towels. The three guards put their uniforms back on, and helped Karl with his.

"You can let the next batch in, now," Klaus said to the guards in the waiting area of the showers. He, Hans, and Wilhelm escorted Karl out the building's rear exit.

As he left, Karl looked up and off to the side to see the girl from the shower crying in the arms of the same older woman with the young daughter, all holding each other, trying to keep warm. The younger teenager, her own cheeks still tear-stained from her experience in the shower room, and the separation from her father, stared at Karl, whispering in her mother's ear, her teeth chattering all the while. All the women waited in the freezing cold, near convulsing from the temperature, dressed in their striped pajamas, for their numerical tattoo.

Karl stopped, fixed his uniform, and straightened his posture. "Okay, my friends, okay." He waved their hands away. "I feel better, now." He still staggered slightly.

"You sure?" asked Wilhelm, giving Karl a serious look. "Did that witch hurt you? We all know about the curses they can lay on us. We could shoot her."

"No, I'm fine, now. I think she'd been trying to curse me since she first saw me by the train. But, we won't shoot her. I think those who go to the left get out too easily. They are devils and, like God did, we've created this Hell just for them, where they belong. All of them should have to endure this as long as possible for their evil deeds. Let God punish them longer for attacking us, our families, our fellow Germans, our way of life. No, they must be made to suffer, as we have suffered at their hands."

"Still," said Klaus, "you should consider having that one disposed of as quickly as possible, since she's such a powerful witch. You couldn't even get yours up, and then you got sick." There was nothing but conviction in his voice.

"I think they were all powerful witches," said Hans. "Why else would we have done what we did with them? I would never touch a Jew. I think they were trying to contaminate our pure blood, or produce witch babies, or something."

"Yes, I saw Klaus pull his gun on his Jew," said Wilhelm.

"Well, she clearly wanted me to shoot all of you, then myself, until I was able to fight against her and point it at her own head. We are all lucky to be alive."

"Thankfully," began Karl, "you had the strength of pure German blood to fend off her attack."

"Karl, I think that you will make camp Kommandant, someday," said Klaus. "You're way too smart not to be."

"A nice thought," said Karl, still stumbling. "I think that for now, however, I should go lie down. I'm heading back to my quarters. I'll see you guys later."

The Camp

"And I think the rest of us are going to get out of this cold, and pick up our drinking where we left off, before we catch pneumonia or something even worse, from these Jew rats."

Karl and Klaus patted each other on the back, and parted ways. Karl began his march through the cold mud of the camp to the SS barracks.

CHAPTER FIVE

Walking through the camp to the guards' barracks, Karl admired the Germans' handiwork. A thin strip of sunlight remained on the horizon, like light coming through the bottom of a closed door, highlighting his way through the bleak workscape.

I'll never be Kommandant of a camp, he thought, responding in secret to Klaus' earlier praise. *These places are good for prisoners, and for Germany, but not for me. If you're so good at running a camp that they make you Kommandant, you'll never leave. That's just another prisoner.*

Even when the sun was as high as it could get in the winter sky, no amount of daylight added any color to the environment of the camp. Everything was gray: the prisoners' striped outfits, the buildings, the guards' uniforms, even the skin of those watched by the guards would, after a time, take on an ashen appearance, which had nothing to do with the constant fleshly snow falling around them from the furnace stacks of the camp crematoria.

It's not that everything in his world was gray; there were the occasional retreats to a nearby, off-site location where he could mingle with officers and female counterparts of the SS. Normally, these invitations were for officers only, but Karl had demonstrated an accelerated rate of potential. Plus, his father wasn't the average party member.

During retreat times, the world was normal, colorful, high in the mountains, surrounded by evergreens and pine trees, covered by blue skies. Wildlife scurried about. There, life blossomed. When he returned to the camp, however, the place where life wilted, withered, and died, the color scheme changed again. As far as any fauna, Karl had never seen a bird, squirrel, or any other creature creep onto the premises. The only animals that roamed the camp, as far as the Nazis were concerned, were the prisoners.

Lost in thought, Karl jumped as he passed a wall and heard a gunshot, followed by the emergence of two laughing guards from behind the partition. Not that he should have jumped at all—the ringing of gunshots was the norm in the camp.

"Did you see how her brains sprayed on the wall?" asked the first man.

"Yeah," laughed the other, "it looked like you threw a tomato at it." He spread his hands apart, demonstrating the explosion on the other side of the wall.

The guards nodded and smiled at Karl as he passed. He nodded back, continuing on, past the prisoners' latrines. Karl didn't have to look to know where he was. He never looked into the exposed area, knowing the amount of feces and urine that often never made it into the open holes on the long wooden plank. He did his best to ignore the smell, but figured it was just part of the job, like a farmer always working around the smell of cattle droppings.

The putrid smell of the waste was okay for the prisoners that had to work the area, okay for Jews, since they were basically the same substance as that which caused the stench, whether they were ordinary inmates or Kapos, but not for someone of his stature, his blood. Besides, everyone knew that what Jews excreted smelled far worse than that of normal people.

Moving past the foul odor of Jew excrement, Karl saw several male prisoners, under armed supervision, finishing up their work for the day. The ongoing construction in the camp seemed less to Karl like functional, structural necessities, and more like measures needed to keep uprisings and riots, like what he'd heard about in the ghettos, from happening. Really, much of it seemed to be just busywork, or something designed to speed the prisoners to their demise.

And this is where the Furor's intelligence shone through, like a beacon for all of Germany to follow: having the demons constantly create, and recreate, their own hell. The guards were simply there to make sure the gates leading from the underworld were never breached. They were angels, the holy few who kept the darkness at bay. Yet, Karl knew, angels had various posts in service to God. He knew the work he was doing was good, and it's not that he didn't enjoy it, but even an angel could be brought down by the constant exposure to such a damning place, the relentless seepage of the sewage in which he worked. This was why he had no interest in being Kommandant.

The Camp

Nearing a building under construction, Karl looked up at the prisoners with their tools, their work continuing as the sun selfishly took what little light remained with it, with one Jew in particular looking ghoulishly thin. He had become good at determining how long, usually to within a week, an inmate had been interred in the camp. Which was how his spending money was usually a little more than the other guards: wagering that he could pinpoint the length of someone's incarceration. Well, more than those guards who weren't able to increase their personal wealth by pilfering from the Nazi party, which increased its own coffers from the individual belongings of the new arrivals to the camp.

And that deterioration, a prisoner's slow demise, was Karl's preferred method of death: long, enduring starvation, and the hopelessness that accompanied it. He knew exactly how long it would take for someone to look like the human skeleton atop the structural skeleton.

He was known throughout the camp for referring to incoming prisoners as Golem, and those who'd been there for some time as zombies. Of all the prisoners contained within the camp—political, gypsy, various nationalities, those considered societal deviants—Karl hated Jews the most.

The current zombie on the top-most perch of the coming building, Karl figured, had been in the camp for three months: the man was incredibly emaciated, his striped uniform hanging loosely from his skeletal frame. He was the thinnest of the prisoners on the construction site. The guards on the ground had him placed atop for a reason—wagering whether the Jew had the wherewithal in his condition to make it back down without falling to his death.

The other construction workers had been incarcerated for a lesser amount of time, but were quickly gaining on the thin man.

"He'll make it down," Karl heard one of the guards say, as he passed the site. "I've seen him up there before. Somehow, he always makes it down. You've heard of the dark horse in a race—that's my dark Jew up there. Get your money ready."

"You're so stupid, Friedrich," said another. "Look at him wobble. He's going to fall at any moment."

"Come on, dark Jew!" yelled the first guard. "You can do it. You'd better do it, if you know what's good for you." The conversation stopped for a few seconds. "See? He's gonna make it."

A second later, a gunshot rang out, followed by the familiar thump of a body hitting the ground. The first guard lost the bet.

"Well, he did make it down," laughed the second guard.

Karl put his hand to his head, the shot still ringing, pounding in his ears. The alcohol coursed through his veins, like the image of the girl in the shower that kept running through his mind.

He closed his eyes tight, trying to rid himself of the moving pictures of the Jew girl, that witch who had entranced him. Yet, she remained.

Her shaven, brown hair; her big, brown eyes; the softness of her skin. He began thinking of other aspects of the moments spent with her, how she felt in other areas of her body, even as he worked desperately to discard those memories. What bothered him most, was that this girl, a Jewish girl, preoccupied his mind.

Some type of hex, he thought. *Clearly she planted a seed in my brain as she tried to get me to plant my seed in her demonic womb.*

He opened his eyes quickly, realizing he was being overcome by dizziness, and about to collide with a wall. The entire camp spun around him. Throwing his arms out, he caught a nearby tree, and remained still, motionless, focusing his eyes on a lone knob of the tree, waiting for the spinning to stop long enough for him to make it to his room.

An officer approached from under the soft glow of the overhead lights, the dark of the night having finally beaten back the last of the sunlight.

"Heil, Hitler!" Karl said, straightening up, throwing his arm out, hoping the man would keep walking. He suddenly felt the urge to regurgitate again, as he had in the shower, belching a couple of times, gagging, sending the taste of vomit to his tastebuds. He held it back.

"Heil, Hitler." The officer continued on, barely looking at Karl.

Approaching the SS barracks located on the other side of the camp, far away from the prisoners, he stumbled into the warm, yellow, three-level, brick-and-mortar building. Shuffling to the second floor and down the hall, Karl entered his room, and walked, zombie-like, to the double-sided, wooden closet along the far wall. He opened the doors, and undressed himself. Losing his balance, he grabbed one door to steady himself, as he removed his pants, but fell nonetheless.

The Camp

Wearing only his white boxers, he pushed his uniform into a pile with his feet, left the closet open, and crawled, ever slowly, to his metal-frame bed. Like a wounded soldier crawling out of a fox hole, he made his way from the floor, and collapsed onto the firm mattress, his head barely missing the wooden nightstand next to his bed. Karl, finally, passed out.

CHAPTER SIX

Rising with the dawn to begin his next shift, Karl made his way out of the SS barracks, and down to breakfast. The biting wind he faced on the way to his morning meal seemed colder than it did the previous night. He watched the smoke from the crematoria chimneys rise, thinking how lucky the SS men were that got to work in such a warm environment.

When he made it to breakfast, and stood in line for his food, the smell of bacon, sausage, and eggs brought the same gagging reflex upon him as the night before. He turned away, and saw his friends sitting at their usual table, looking no worse for wear. Knowing he still needed to eat something, he grabbed some eggs, and proceeded to the middle of the mess hall.

Karl's temples throbbing from the previous night's drinking, he seemed distracted as he sat at the square wooden table with his scrambled eggs, and fellow guards. It took several minutes for him to realize that Hans, Klaus, and Wilhelm were snickering at him.

"What?" asked Karl. "I'm not in the mood today."

"You're so serious all the time, you're never in the mood," said Klaus. "Your uniform looks a little wrinkled. Same one from last night?"

"So?" Karl looked at Hans and Wilhelm, both still snickering. "What's so damn funny?"

"Your hair's messed up, too," said Hans. "You want to use my comb?"

"Okay, forget the damn uniform and comb," Klaus continued. "Let's move on. You talked to anyone else this morning, Karl?"

"No. Who else would I talk to? Why do you ask?"

"Well, it's just that there's an interesting little rumor circulating."

"A rumor? Does it look like I care about rumors, right now?"

"No, but, this one's *really* interesting."

"Get to the point, Klaus. My head is killing me. The next time I drink Jaeger, Himmler himself better be serving it to me."

"Tell him," said Hans, his eagerness to exploit whatever secret the group had, written all over his face.

"Tell me what?" Karl tapped his fork on the table. "What's the rumor?"

"It's no rumor," said Wilhelm. "I saw him, myself."

"Saw who?" Karl asked, growing more impatient. "Get to the fucking point."

"Apparently," began Klaus, "there's a prisoner here, a *Jewish* prisoner, who looks like you. More like you than someone should look."

"Yeah, right, and Marlene Dietrich is working over in Kanada."

"It's true, Karl," said Wilhelm. "I saw him."

Karl slammed his fork down, getting the attention of senior SS officers sitting across the dining hall. "Piss off, Wilhelm! You haven't seen anyone!"

"Calm down," said Klaus. "You're drawing attention."

"But, I have," Wilhelm whispered, leaning halfway over table. "I saw him myself. He came in on the train last night, the one with the girls, you know?"

"Look," Karl began, his face reddening, "for a Jew to look like me, that means that I have to look like him. Do I look like a Golem to you? You've all seen The Eternal Jew, you've seen the diagrams, do I look like that? Do I have a misshapen head, or crooked nose? Do I smell like a Jew?"

"No."

"You're all walking a thin line, my friends. You want to compare me to a rat? To a Jew? The two creatures that brought the plague to Europe? To a parasite that survives off its host organism? Those parasites from last night have gotten into your brains. I'm the only one protected because I'm the only one who didn't--."

"Keep your voice down," said Klaus, his voice lowered. "Those officers are *still* looking over here. No one's supposed to know about last night. I'm sure Wilhelm, and everyone else, is mistaken. And stop rubbing your education in our faces. Not all of us have your father's money."

"What do you mean, 'everyone else'?"

"Like I said, it's a rumor moving through the guards."

"Then, I will squash this rumor now."

Karl got up, and marched to the exit, followed by his three friends.

The Camp

"What are you doing?" asked Klaus. "We can't just leave our food on the table."

Stopping outside, Karl looked around the camp, scanning the area. Nothing eventful was happening: prisoners were working, and guards patrolled fences. Karl, however, was snapping inside. His head, and his pride, ached. He needed an outlet.

Finally, he locked his sights onto one individual. Turning around to see his friends, and the senior officers that had followed the entire group out, Karl smiled, and continued on his march.

He walked to a far point in the fence that separated the men from the women. There, he found a man, interred for a day or two Karl surmised, gesturing with his hands to a woman on the other side of the camp. He looked up at the guard in the tower that stood only yards away.

"What the hell are you doing?" yelled Karl.

It took the guard a couple of seconds, but he finally saw his fellow Nazi on the ground, realizing he was yelling at him.

"What do you mean?" the tower guard yelled back.

"These two prisoners are communicating. And you're just letting it happen?"

"I'm sorry, but I didn't hear them."

"They're talking with their hands, moron, in secret Jew code. You're supposed to be watching as well as listening."

Karl turned his attention again to the prisoner at the fence. "Turn around, Jew," he said.

The man kept gesturing, neither turning nor responding. Karl looked at the female recipient of the Jewish code, noting the fear in her face. He saw her point at him.

"What the fuck are you doing with your hands? I said turn around, Jew. And, tell that Jew bitch to stop pointing at me."

The man suddenly dropped his hands to his side. Karl noticed the woman made quick movements with hers, and stopped.

The prisoner slowly turned around, and lowered his gaze to the ground.

"So, you speak in code with your fellow prisoners, and ignore me. Not very smart is it?"

The man said nothing.

"Please," yelled the woman across the way. "He cannot hear you. He meant no disrespect."

"Cannot hear? A deaf rat? Why, however did you escape the attention of our esteemed doctors? You should have already met your fate. I shall have to remedy that, immediately."

Karl backhanded the deaf man, pulled his pistol before the prisoner could right himself, and struck him with the butt of the weapon. With one quick blow to the side of the head, Karl's target fell to the ground.

"Please!" the woman on the other side of the fence yelled. "Please, stop! I will not talk to him anymore! No, my Josef!"

Fueled by the woman's screams, Karl unleashed his anger on the man in the striped outfit.

Straddling the Jewish prisoner, the Nazi delivered blow after blow to the man's head, spurts of red spraying the guard's gray uniform. The prisoner held his hands up, attempting to block the attack, screaming in a muted tone.

"Tell me," Karl yelled at the woman, "how did he know what to do when he was given a command? How did he go unnoticed?"

"He can read lips. He's very intelligent. I'm sure he would be a hard worker for you."

"An intelligent Jew?" Karl laughed. "I doubt it."

Karl stood, firing one shot into each arm, forcing his victim to drop his defenses. Back down the Nazi went, continuing his rampage, looking over to the other fence to see the woman on her knees, pleading for him to stop.

Karl stripped the prisoner of his striped outfit, taking what little warmth the man had, exacerbating his pain by exposing his open wounds to the bitter cold wind.

"This is how we take care of rats!" yelled Karl.

Karl stood once more, and fired a single shot to the naked man's chest, missing his heart, though still supplying a grave wound.

"Now," Karl said to the woman, "you can watch him die slowly."

Half attempting to rub the blood off his clothes, Karl looked at his friends, and the smiling officers that stood behind them, as he walked by.

"Looks like you were right," he said to Klaus and the other guards. "I do need to change uniforms for the day."

He holstered his pistol, and walked back to his barracks.

CHAPTER SEVEN

1993

The FBI's interrogation room erupted, as the old woman, Karl's accuser, burst into hysterics.

"I knew it was you!" she screamed, her entire body trembling. "You killed him! You killed my Josef!"

The old woman tried reaching across the cold, steel table, clawing the air to get to Karl, who did his best to sit motionless, only his wavy white hair moving in the wind of the woman's swipes.

"Get her out of here!" said Agent Williams.

"What a horrible way for him to die! And, I…I was forced to dig a ditch for my dead husband! His body lay next to me and I had to dig his hole!"

Karl kept silent.

"You will get what's coming to you!" she continued. "All those lives destroyed! All those people! The babies!"

"Agent Stein," said Williams, "get her out! Now!"

"Josef! Josef! My Josef!"

Stein grabbed the woman by her shoulders, pulling her gently back, off the table, and out the door. Upon their departure from the room, Williams again turned his attention to the old man.

"Well," Williams began, "looks like you were wrong, Mister Engel. You will be standing trial for crimes against humanity, and for at least one particular murder."

"No, I'm not."

"How do you figure? You just implicated yourself in a homicide. One that took place over fifty years ago, but your admission counts, nonetheless."

"I did not implicate myself. At least, not in relation to crimes against humanity, not war crimes. Those types of charges stipulate that I am guilty of the most horrendous and heinous acts. Of course, one could argue that any murder, even one, is a crime against humanity."

Agent Williams sat down, furrowing his brows, a perplexing look of bewilderment on his face. He bent over, lowering his head to his hands, massaging his face, and raised back up.

"You just said that Karl Engel killed a man in a Nazi concentration camp in…," he fumbled through his notes, "here it is, in February, Nineteen Forty-Three, correct?"

"Yes."

Williams again looked at the old man with confusion.

"Your name is Karl Engel, correct?"

"Yes."

Agent Williams stood, grabbing his notes and a file folder. "Sir, I think it's time I order a psych-eval."

"You can order one of your lie detector tests, if you like. But you need to let me continue my story."

"Pop," Aaron interjected, stepping into the room, "don't say anything else, please."

"Son, I hadn't even noticed you weren't in here. How long have you been in the hall?"

"Not long." Karl's son motioned for a well-dressed man in his mid-thirties to enter the room. "This is my lawyer."

"Hello, Mister Engel. I'm Robert Genero." The attorney stuck one hand out for a handshake, and with the other, wiped his brow with a white handkerchief pulled from his pocket. "Hot out there today, isn't it?" He received no handshake in return.

"Yes, I've seen your commercials on television," said Karl. "You're the one who always rides on elephants, saying you'll bring order to the circus of Louisville's court system. Usually, though, people just make fun of you, calling you the Clown of the Courts."

Genero set his black briefcase on the table. "Yes, well, I'd advise you to take your son's, and my, advice and say nothing else."

"Excuse me," said Agent Williams, "but he's already waived his right to an attorney."

"I believe that, according to what his son has told me, Mister Engel is not of sound mind. In fact, he may be suffering from dementia. And the one witness you *do* have wants to implicate my client based on a name and description from fifty years ago."

"Sir," said Karl, "I am not your client. I did not hire you."

"Besides," said Williams, "he's already confessed, kind of, so your services are not needed, Mister Genero."

"A confession under mental duress means nothing."

"He's under no duress, mental or otherwise," Agent Williams said, growing noticeably irritated. "As you can see, he's not even cuffed."

"Pop, you've said too much as it is, about things you know nothing about."

"It's too late for that, son. The time to tell the story is now, before something happens to me. It needs to be heard."

"Well," said Williams, "I think I've heard enough." He pushed his chair up to the table, and moved toward the door.

"You've heard nothing. There is much more to tell."

"Mister Engel, you have no hope of escaping judgment."

"Mister Williams, you will be surprised at the places, and times, in which one can find hope."

Williams stopped with the door halfway open. The old woman could be heard crying down the hall. He looked at Aaron, Karl's son, and the attorney, Robert Genero.

"If you're so sure," said Karl, "that I will stand trial for these crimes, the war crimes, then it hurts no one for me to finish the story. You will lose only a couple of hours, but will be remembered as one of the few men in history to bring to justice a real Nazi criminal. However, just like before, I must insist that the woman, and Agent Stein, be present. The lawyer can go."

"You can't be serious," said Williams. "After what you just put her through? After what you just saw?"

"I must insist."

Agent Williams squinted, staring at Karl. "Okay. Fine. I'll bring them in."

"Mister Engel," said Genero, "I highly advise you not to do this."

"You are not my counsel, and are free to go at any time."

"Sir," Aaron said to Williams, "may I have a moment alone with my dad?"

"Sure. I'll refill my coffee, and grab the others. Be back in a few minutes."

"Well," said Genero, "I will not be here. Good day to you, Mister Engel, and good luck in your endeavor to be tried for war crimes in Germany, or Poland, or wherever it is they want to send you." Robert Genero took his black briefcase, and walked out the door.

Karl's son waited for the door to close then leaned in toward his father.

"What are you doing?" he asked. "Why are you saying these things? I know you didn't do any of this. You were never anywhere near a concentration camp."

"Son, like everyone else in this room, you know nothing about me. And, I'm very sorry for that. You carry the name Engel, and today, you will shoulder the burden, as I have, that comes with that name."

"Pop," Aaron said, placing his hand on his father's, "tell me you didn't really do any of those things. Tell me you were never involved in any killings in one of those camps."

"I'm sorry, but I can't tell you that I didn't kill anyone in a death camp, because I was there, and I know what I did. I am guilty of murder."

Aaron, sat back, a grave look on his face. He and his father sat quietly, saying nothing, for the next ten minutes, until the silence was finally broken by Agent Williams reentering the room, followed by Agent Stein and the old woman, the wife of the man killed fifty years earlier.

"Please, ma'am, sit down," Karl said to her.

"I will stay and face you, when my husband cannot," she said.

"I can't wait for you to finish so I can personally escort you to the plane that will take you to justice," said Stein.

"Mister Engel," Williams began, "this day has been very emotional, very taxing for everyone here, but we have all returned as you have requested. Please, make it worth our while." Williams took his seat, placing his notes back on the table. "You may continue."

CHAPTER EIGHT

1943

Having changed into a crisp, clean uniform, Karl approached, quietly, like a shadow, the area of the camp where his doppelganger was known to be incarcerated. He had to see this man for himself. He'd asked around about the prisoner who looked like him, where he was being kept, and Karl soon found him, exactly where he was told the man would be—cleaning the latrines.

As Karl moved closer, the verbal taunts coming from the Kapo assigned to the man's group sang sweetly in his ears. He stopped before reaching his destination, and stood back, watching from a hidden vantage point.

"Let's go, monkey!" yelled the Kapo. "You people shit enough around here to stink up all of Poland!"

It didn't matter to Karl that the Kapo was also one of the *people* the guy was talking about, a Jew; the roles of Kapo and prisoner provided an interesting state of poetic irony. It was another way of subjugating the populace, like the use of overseers on plantations of the old American South. It was also another way of exerting the Nazis' power, and humiliating and breaking the prisoners down mentally, by having one of their own push aside his or her own morals and ethics for the sake of their personal survival.

Karl found it interesting that the Kapos could be just as cruel, if not more so, than the Nazis. He despised the Jews, but it was the Kapos who disgusted him the most, for they represented everything that there was to hate about the Jewish people—those who would turn on their own kind, or anyone else for that matter, for their own self-serving purposes. The Kapos received better food, clothing, and a place to sleep, all for the job of mistreating other Jews. For Karl, only these bipedal rats behaved in such a way.

Several male prisoners were working under this particular Kapo's work detail at the moment, cleaning their own toilets. One of the prisoners, his bucket too heavy to carry for his emaciated body, tripped, spilling the contents all over the ground.

"You stupid fuck!" yelled the Kapo, a short man with dark hair. He walked over to the Jew on the ground, still struggling to get up, his hands in the filth he'd just spilled.

The Kapo kicked the man twice, and on the third time, pushed the prisoner's entire body into the sewage that was now mixing with the mud. The other Jews in the work detail continued about their business, carrying their buckets, like ants moving to and from a picnic buffet, the contents sometimes slopping out onto the striped outfits.

"Now, look at you," said the Kapo. "You're a mess. And I'm going to be down one Jew for the day's work. You miserable shit, they should have killed you when you first got here."

Karl watched the other Jews in the work procession, until he spotted the one he was looking for. From a distance, the man vaguely resembled himself, but it was enough that the Nazi felt he needed to take a closer look. Karl stepped out from the shadow of the building that was hiding him, and walked toward the Kapo.

"Maybe you should be the one in the bucket," the Kapo continued, suddenly stiffening his body in a sort of attention stance when Karl came into view.

"Cleaning latrines, are we?" Karl asked.

"Yes, sir."

"Hmm, excrement cleaning excrement. How does that work?"

The Kapo laughed nervously then stopped when Karl leered at him.

"I want that Jew," Karl said, pointing at the man on his way back to the latrine area after emptying his bucket.

"Yes, sir." The Kapo sprinted toward the prisoner, yelling obscenities and striking him in the back to get him to move quicker.

Karl took several steps back as the prisoner approached, overwhelmed by the stench emanating from him. "You smell worse than you normally would," he said.

The prisoner kept his eyes on the ground.

"Look at me," said Karl, to the man in the usually black and white, but now brown-stained, outfit. "Kapo, leave us."

Karl, his hand acting as a mask on the lower half of his face to block the smell, focused his attention solely on the man in front of him.

The dark, shorn hair, and deep blue eyes did look strangely familiar. The height was the same, but the weight was a little off, which Karl quickly attributed to the food rations in whichever ghetto the man came from.

The guard walked around the prisoner, noting the broad shoulders, wide stance, thin neck, and back around to the face—small nose and ears, thin lips. Every feature the same as his own. Then he noticed the prisoner scanning the face of the guard that stood before him.

"Don't look at me," Karl said. "Did I give you permission to eyeball me?"

"No, sir." The man returned his gaze to the mud at his feet.

"Your name, Jew, what is it?"

"Albert, sir. Albert Fogel."

"Who are you?"

"Albert, sir--."

"Not your name again, you filthy, stinking rat, I mean who are you? Why do you look like me?"

"I don't know what you mean, sir."

"Yes, you do. That's why you were looking at me. How did you do it, Albert Fogel? How did you make yourself look not only human, but like another human? I know you Jews are adept at fitting in with society, looking like everyone else, so no one knows what you really are, but to look like someone who already exists—that's a new kind of sorcery. Was it the witch from the shower?"

"Who, sir?"

Karl paused, studying the man, as if in a game of poker, waiting for him to expose his hand. The man stood motionless, silent.

"Nevermind."

Seconds passed, until the prisoner spoke up. "I'm sorry, sir, but I don't know why you look like me."

"Look like you?" screamed Karl, the boiling point of his blood reaching a new record time. "I do not look like you, like a Jew! You have disguised yourself, to infiltrate this camp, and take my place!"

Karl took a step back then thrust his right leg out, kicking Albert to the ground.

"You want to be me?" said Karl, kicking Albert again, sending him back into the feces-mixed mud, as he tried to rise. "Feel what it's like to be me!"

Karl kicked Albert repeatedly, the sound of his foot contacting with Albert's body resonating for several yards. From the prisoner's underside, to his back, then his head, Karl hit every spot he could. The cold mud underneath changed from a dark brown to a warm red.

Albert screamed, begged, pleaded for Karl to stop, which only incensed the Nazi further, until Karl finally cracked his living mirror, hearing the fallen man's ribs break.

Karl walked over to the same building under construction from the previous night, and grabbed a two-by-four.

"Whatever you did to look like me, I'm about to remedy."

Suddenly, Klaus rushed in between the two men, throwing his hands up, and stopping Karl in his tracks.

"What are you doing?" asked Karl. "Saving him?"

"You know me better than that," Klaus said. "Sorry to bother you, but the officers from this morning, the ones from the dining hall, who saw you kill the deaf Jew, want to see you."

"Can't it wait?" Karl said in a huff, still eyeing Albert. "I'm a little busy at the moment. Look, Klaus, I found that sneaking Jew you were talking about. And, just like you guys, he said I look like him. That I look like a Jew."

"Yes, I see that you found him. And, as much as I would enjoy standing here and watching you continue, I wouldn't make the officers wait. They said it was very important and to bring you back immediately. You can come back to him; he's not going anywhere."

Karl, breathing heavy, dropped the wood plank, straightened his uniform, and motioned for other nearby prisoners, the latrine ants, to retrieve Albert.

"We'll finish this later, Judenscheisse," said Karl as he was led away, watching the ants carry the bloody, broken pulp of a body to their barracks.

"Well," Klaus began, "do you see the resemblance?"

"No. I don't see it at all."

CHAPTER NINE

The following morning, Karl stood in the cold, dawn air, trying to absorb any warmth he could from the uncharitable Polish sun. He waited at his post by the train tracks, watching the coming transport full of new arrivals approach in the distance.

"Hey, Karl."

The guard turned to see Klaus coming up from behind. "What?"

"Did you finish your business with your double from yesterday? What was your meeting with the officers about anyway? What was so important?"

"No, I never got back to him after I met with them. I'd lost my interest by that point, but I do plan on paying him a visit later today—if you know what I mean. He probably thinks he got out of anymore trouble because I didn't come back. Well, let him keep on thinking it, until I round a corner, heading his way. As far as what the meeting was about, I'm getting a commodation."

"Hey, that's good to hear!"

"Yeah, it is."

"Next, you'll be getting a personal meeting with the Fuhrer in Berlin. Just don't forget about us little people."

Karl laughed. "I won't."

"Well, I gotta get back to work. I was just curious about all that." Klaus turned to leave, when he suddenly stopped. "Oh, I almost forgot, one of the female prisoners wants to see you."

Karl's mind immediately rushed to the night in the shower. "What does she look like?"

"A Jew." Klaus gave Karl a strange look. "What do you think she looks like?" Klaus shook his head as he began walking off. "We started to shoot her just for asking a question," he continued over his departing shoulder, "you know, first asking if she could ask a question, then making the request to see you, but then we figured it'd be worse for her if we actually gave her what she wanted—you."

"Where is she?"

"C Barracks," said Klaus, rounding a corner, out of sight.

Karl motioned for a nearby guard, a fresh recruit, to stand in his spot, instructing him to get the Jews off the train as quickly as possible, separate the men from the women and children, yell at any that spoke, and let the doctor do the rest.

Moments later, entering 'C' Barracks on the women's side of the camp, Karl walked past the stacks of wood-framed bunk beds, three beds to a stack, that filled the building. Each bed provided a place to sleep for three prisoners. The odor that hit him upon his entrance was horrendous, like hundreds of bodies, already dead, all rotting together. Except that they weren't dead—not yet.

Half-way down the aisle, he found the older woman from the other night, the one who had comforted the young woman immediately after the shower incident, sitting on her bunk. She was flanked on either side by the same woman who was now returning the favor, and the older woman's teenage daughter, the young girl who kept staring at Karl that night, and who had called out for her dad. The only one he saw now, though, the only one he cared to see, was the girl from the shower. He watched her tremble, her tremors increasing the closer he got. The older woman grabbed the girl's hand, and squeezed.

"What do you need?" he asked, never moving his gaze from the young woman's brown eyes.

"I am the one that asked for you," said the older woman, her dark hair looking as if it were graying before its time, belying the compacted stress and wear the woman's mind and body seemed to be under.

Karl broke his focus. "You? Well, I'm here. What do you want? I'm a very busy man."

"I want to speak with you, alone."

"You want to be left alone with me?"

"I'm not scared of you," she said.

"Obviously, my reputation has not gotten this far in the camp, yet," he said, disappointed. "Very well." He turned his attention back to the two younger women. "Leave us."

"Mom?" said the youngest girl.

The Camp

"It's okay," the older woman said, looking up at Karl. "I'll be alright."

"Where's my dad?" the girl asked Karl.

Karl bent down, closer to the pretty mid-teen with high cheekbones and an overbite, asking menacingly, "Your father was the man with the clubhand, the one that started in one direction the other night, and ended up going down another, right?"

"Yes."

"Not now," said her mother. "Just go. Everything's going to be okay. We'll talk later."

"You know," said Karl, watching the girls leave, "I admire your courage, but you should be scared of me. You haven't been here long, but you'll soon learn all about me."

A few tears ran down the woman's face as she stared at Karl.

"Ah, there's the fear I was hoping to see," he said.

"I do not cry out of fear of you, but out of love for someone who's been hurt. I already know all about you. Word travels fast among the prisoners. Your reputation has gotten farther than you think, but I'm not scared."

Karl smiled. "So you have heard what I'm capable of, yet you have no fear of me. You're an interesting Jew. What else do you know?"

"I know you will never have a chance at Else."

"Else?"

"The young woman you keep staring at, the woman you traumatized the other night. To her, your cruelty outweighs your humanity."

"Ah, so that's her name. You know her?"

"Of course, I know her; we are stuck here together, where it seems Yahweh has turned His back on us both. But, I've known her for quite some time. We are from the same neighborhood, in Germany, and were later sent to the same ghetto, in Poland."

"Well, I don't know what she told you," he said, growing angry, "but I didn't do anything to her. She hexed me. And what do you know of humanity? You're not even human?"

"Why did you kill that man, the one who could not hear you?"

"What concern is that of yours? Is that what you wanted to know, why I kill vermin?" He watched her eyes well again, though never looking away. "Are you afraid now?"

45

"No, I am not."

"Why not? Are you so stupid that you think I will not kill a woman? I—we—kill more than Jews, you know."

"Like who? You seem so proud of it."

"I am proud of it, to rid my country of the weak, and those who burden and poison the rest of us."

"Who do you kill besides Jews?"

"Gypsies, homosexuals, retarded people—all kinds." He answered her question with a certain amount of flair in his voice. "Those who are less than."

"Less than? Less than what?"

"Less than pure German," he said, astounded at the stupidity of the question.

"That's why you killed the deaf man?"

Karl rested his hand against his holstered pistol, making sure the woman could see the gesture. "Am I being interrogated? Be careful with your answer. I'm in a good mood, but I can also be turned quickly."

"No, I am not interrogating you. I simply want to understand."

"You will never understand," he said, laughing, "because you lack the capacity to understand, but, yes, I killed that man because he was less than pure, less than whole, and I was angry. I needed to relieve my anger. He also didn't respond when he should have. He shouldn't have made it as far as he had in the first place."

"Did you enjoy killing someone?"

"I didn't kill *someone*, I killed a rat—a pest, vermin. An animal. I enjoyed it as much as any hunter would."

"Was it your first time?"

"I am quickly losing my patience with these questions. I really don't know why I'm bothering to answer any of them at all. I should kill you just on principle."

Tears streamed down her cheeks. "Why did you nearly kill that young man, yesterday?"

"So, good news does travel fast among your kind. Well, yesterday's business, now that was a completely different reason. Tell me woman, what does it matter to you? I remember your daughter asking about her father that night, but I don't recall any connection between you and this other Jew. And why *are* you asking me all these damn questions? What is it you want? Why did you really ask to speak to me?"

"I know why you beat him, the young man from yesterday. What I don't know is why you didn't kill him."

"You know nothing, Jew witch." Karl began making his way back down the aisle and out the barracks. "I didn't kill him because I was interrupted, but I'll be finishing the job, soon enough."

"I know more than you think," she said. "I know you beat him because he looks like you. And, I know why he does…look like you."

Karl froze in his tracks, did an about face, and hurried back to her bunk.

"How do you know him?" he screamed, grabbing her by her time-worn cheeks, pulling her off her bed. Karl towered over her five-foot-three-inch frame. "I will beat you right here, just for saying that. I should kill you. I was glad I was interrupted in killing him, so that I could experience the joy of doing it all over again later."

"You may have been interrupted, but you're also curious about him. That's why you haven't gone back and finished before now. And, I told you, I'm not afraid of you."

"You are both brave, and foolish, Jew bitch. Now tell me, how do you know him?"

"He's my son."

Karl released her, and took a couple steps back. "Your son?" He squinted at her blue eyes. "What is his name?"

"Albert."

"And what is your name?"

"My name is Miriam, Miriam Fogel. My daughter's name is Sarah."

"Why did you tell me her name? I didn't ask you that. What I really want to know, though, is why your Jew son looks like me?"

Her arms jerked slightly outward, as if she wanted to touch him, but held back. The corners of her mouth curled down, tears streaming from both eyes.

"The reason he looks like you is the same reason why I do not fear you." The woman stood, moving closer to Karl as he backed away, her blue eyes locked onto his. "I will never fear my son—neither him, or you."

CHAPTER TEN

Karl stumbled back, grabbed the nearest bunk to steady himself, only to collapse to the floor.

"You lie," he whispered. "This is a Jew trick."

"You know I'm not lying," she said, sitting on the lowest bunk next to him, crying uncontrollably, overcome with emotion, her voice straining. "Please, forgive me. I know that everything you're going to hear is a shock for you, but this is the first time that I've seen you since I gave birth to you eighteen years ago, the first time I've been able to talk to you." She stopped to catch her breath, wiping her eyes, which only released more tears the more she wiped. "I want so much to reach out and touch you. I want so much just to hold you, again."

"Don't you dare touch me," said Karl, jerking back, disgusted. "You lying Jews are not fit to touch me. You don't put your hands on this uniform."

"I'm sorry," she continued, drawing back. "Anyway, you know I'm right. You've seen for yourself. You've seen your twin brother. I am your mother, Albert is your brother, Sarah is your sister, and Jakob…," Miriam's voice trailed off. She turned her head.

"Who the hell is Jakob?"

"The man from the other night, Sarah's father, the one with the clubhand. You and the doctor sent him to the left. No one has seen him, or anyone else who went in that direction, since. I assume the worst. Am I right?"

"Yes, you are. But, what you're saying is that he was…"

"Yes, he was your father."

Karl suddenly came to another realization. He felt his face burn.

"If you are my mother, and you are a Jew, that means--." Karl stopped himself before the sentence could be completed, doing his best to keep the words from forming even in his mind.

Miriam remained quiet.

"You lie!" Karl jumped to his feet, grabbing her by the shoulder and lifting her off the bunk to face him. "I am no damn Jew! I will have you shot for this! Your whole family will go to the chamber!"

Suddenly, Karl drew his gun, and pressed the cold barrel against Miriam's forehead. "Say it! Admit that you are lying! You are lying, and you're going to die for it!"

He searched Miriam's eyes for fear, for a sign that would tell him that she was, in fact, lying. Any shift in her demeanor. He found only sadness.

"Pull the trigger," she said. "I am already dead in such a place. We all are. Even you, my son. No one who works here will ever be free from its reach."

The weapon shook in Karl's hand. His breathing was heavy, quick, and erratic. He cocked the gun. Karl closed his eyes, and turned his head away, the barrel digging into her skin.

Suddenly, Karl jerked the pistol away, resetting it, let go of Miriam, and fell back to the floor. He said nothing.

"What is the chamber?" she asked, returning to her bunk. "Is it a cell? Is that where Jakob went?"

Karl could only sit on the cold floor, one hand to his head, the other holding his pistol.

"We tried to protect our other children, Albert and Sarah, but that is difficult to do when the entire country is out to get them."

Karl still sat quiet, feeling nauseous. Growing light-headed, he repositioned himself on his knees, and doubled over. His damp uniform clung to his sweat-diffused body.

"I'm sorry," she said. "Sorry that I am partly responsible for the man you are today. When you were born, you were very sick. You had trouble breathing, and your arms and legs would not move, as if you were paralyzed. We would not have given you up so easily, but the doctor said that your condition was permanent, and that the quality of care you would have received if you had stayed with us would have been so low. He said that you would have a better chance elsewhere.

"A non-Jewish couple, friends of ours, who were sympathetic to us, took you to a non-Jewish orphanage so that no one would suspect what you really were. In fact, we, and I don't mean to embarrass you, but we had you moved before you were eight days old, so that you would not have been circumcised. We believed that you would get better care somewhere else. The couple that helped us didn't even tell anyone at the orphanage that you were a twin. We did the best we could to give you the best chance at any decent life. I never told your brother, or sister, about you. I was hoping I could give you a better life and, to some degree, I was right, but I also see that I still failed.

"I've missed you every day for the past eighteen years," she continued. "You were always the missing piece in our lives. Sometimes, I would catch Jakob, sitting alone, crying. I knew why he cried, because I cried, too, when I was alone. We never knew what happened to you, never knew what became of our other child. We didn't know you were taken in by people with such hatred in their hearts."

Karl's temper again burst forth.

"Shut up! Your doctor was obviously wrong, since I was never paralyzed as a child, and there's nothing wrong with me today. I was never hospitalized, so, clearly, I was misdiagnosed.

"And, you don't know anything about my parents. They raised me to be a proud German, teaching me what it's like to have honor, to put my country first. I got to go to the best schools, get the best education, because of my father, my *real* father, and his connections. If what you say is true, which I don't believe it is, at least they cared enough to take me in, and keep me. At least, they wanted, and loved, me."

"I loved you," she pleaded. "I have always loved you. Yes, obviously the doctor was wrong, you got better. But, I didn't know. Do you think it was easy to give you up? To let someone else have my child, my baby? Even today, Karl, I love you, even with you being the man that you are. And, I can see that you have been educated, I can hear it when you speak. But, whoever took you in did not show you love, or how to love; they showed you only hate."

"There's nothing wrong with the man I am today. Why are you even telling me all of this today? Why didn't you just keep it to yourself?"

"Because, there *is* something wrong, Karl—your cruelty, your hatred for others, your violent ways—none of that would be in you now if I had kept you. You are my son, and you are lost. I am responsible for that, and I am trying to save you. You don't have to be this person. You can still be saved. Please, let me help you."

"Save me? I'm being given a commendation for all of those *violent ways*. What you call cruelty, hatred, and violent, we call honor, loyalty, and preservation of the pure German way of life. That's why I was interrupted when dealing with your son—my superiors wanted to reward me for killing the deaf man. Does that sound like I need saving?" Karl paused. "You say I don't have to be this person, but you don't know what I have to be." He looked her straight in the eye. "Some people have their destinies thrust upon them by others."

"You are being rewarded for killing another human being?"

"You people are not human!" he snapped, rising to his feet, separating himself once again. "You're sub-human!"

"Yet," she said, "you now know that you are one of those sub-humans."

Karl suddenly slapped Miriam, knocking her from the bunk to the floor.

"You can strike me all you want, but you now know that Jewish blood runs in your veins; that your heart is Jewish," she continued. "I wonder, do you enjoy what you do? Is there any part of you that tells you that what you are doing here, in this place, is all wrong?"

Karl steadied himself against a bed. He had to concentrate to keep from swaying on his weakened legs. He left her question unanswered.

"What will you do now?" she asked, from the floor. "Are you going to turn us in? Send us, your family, to your chamber?"

"You are not my family," he said, keeping his back to her. "I don't believe you. You and your Jewish friends have isolated me from my real brothers, my pure comrades, in order to try to place another hex on me." Karl turned to face her. "You want to know what the chamber is? I'll tell you.

"It's a shower room," he continued, drawing closer to her, feeding off the horror on her face, "like the one you were in your first night here, except this one, instead of water pouring on you from above, fills the air with gas. We tell you that you are here to work, that you will be fed, that you may be free, one day. Then, because you are scared, and hold onto hope, you believe us, and so you go into the showers, without any trouble. Then, we lock you in the room. Two guards stand on the roof above, open the lids, and drop the gas pellets down. That's when you discover that you are about to die. But, it's not a quick death, no. It takes several minutes, and you scream and scratch at the walls, at the doors, trying to get out."

Karl stood erect, straightened his uniform, and headed toward the door. Before exiting, however, he stopped, turning his head toward his shoulder, listening to her cry.

"And, that's exactly where your husband went," he said as he finally walked out.

CHAPTER ELEVEN

Having requested, and received, two days off, Karl drove down the scenic German road to his parents' house, not far from the country's border with Poland. The rising star at the camp had no trouble persuading his superiors in providing a couple of personal days. He'd told them he wanted to tell his father personally about all the good work he'd been doing and his commendation.

"Take one of the camp's Kubelwagens," said the Kommandant from behind his desk, throwing Karl a set of keys.

"But, sir," began Karl, "I'm not sure I should--."

"Nonsense. You're really coming up in the Nazi ranks, and your father is an important man. It will only impress him further, the fact that your camp's Kommandant trusts you with one of the vehicles, to drive it out of the country. I see a bright future for you, Engel."

Heinrich Engel's estate lay at the end of a long, idyllic tree-lined drive in the German countryside. Driving the beige vehicle down the lane, tiny Nazi flags attached to the front flapping in the wind, the bolted spare tire vibrating on the hood, Karl thought back on the child he used to be, pretending he was a World War One soldier, picking invisible enemies off, one-by-one, as they jumped out at him from behind the hedges that filled in the gaps between the trees. Now, he was a man, helping to kill more people than he ever imagined.

He pulled the car into the semi-circular drive in front of the white, two-story mansion, and got out. Nazi banners hung between windows, stretching from the top of one story, to the bottom of the other.

"Hello, son," said his father, coming out in a stately manner to greet his son, his cold-blue eyes piercing Karl's soul. The elder Engel's tall, broad physique provided those on the outside a good impression of the stern man that lay within. His perfectly coifed graying hair still contained streaks of the blond that used to be.

Karl's mother, Olga, followed, her yellow dress, draped past her knees, matching her still-blonde hair.

"Father," Karl said.

"It's good to see you, son." Heinrich shot his hand out, giving his son a good, firm handshake. "I've been working on designing a new building for the party, to be built in eastern Poland, near those damned Soviets. My work has steadily increased since my input into the designs of various camps." He walked over to the Kubelwagen, looking inside the vehicle. "Well, I can see that you are becoming someone, as well. But, tell me, what is so important that you feel the need to leave your job for the day? You know how important I feel work is."

"I got two days off, actually. Yes, sir, I know what work means to you. I'll be here today, and tomorrow I'll be going to Berlin. It's a kind of personal celebration." Karl's eyes scanned the mansion's manicured grounds, moving around the premises until they fell to his mother. "You know, this place is so big, I never understood why you've never hired a maid, or butler, or someone to help around here."

"Why would I? Your mother does such a fine job of doing everything that needs to be done. Remember, when you get married—Kinder, Kuche, Kirche. That's how it should be. Now, this trip, this personal celebration of yours, does not pertain to work?"

"Well, I'm not on any kind of assignment, so not really."

"Then it is an unwise venture," said Heinrich in a scolding tone. "I did not raise you, Karl, to just take off from service to your country whenever you feel the urge."

"I know father, but I wanted to give you and mother some good news before I go to Berlin to see how our great Fuhrer has transformed the city since my last visit."

"Hmm." Heinrich squinted, though the day was cloudy, seemingly judging everything Karl was saying. "A proud German, you are, Karl. I am pleased to hear it. In that case, please, sit with us and tell us your news. I will show you my new design, and you will regale us with your news. You must be doing well in your assignment to have a requested leave, and have it granted so quickly."

The Camp

Heinrich motioned for Olga and Karl to move inside, out of the cold February air.

Inside, Karl's father escorted his son to his study, where several blueprints lay spread across a large, oak desk.

"What is it?" Karl asked. Even without an engineer's education, he could see that, whatever he was looking at, it was massive in scale.

"A new camp," Heinrich said. "One which will dwarf all others. It'll be the size of several of what we have now, combined."

"But, why so big?"

"Karl," sighed Heinrich, "why do you ask such stupid questions? Once this war is over, we will need a place large enough to kill not only the remainder of the world's Jews, but all other enemies of the State. Why do you think it's so close to the Soviet border?" The older man tapped his finger on the schematics. "See this building here?"

Karl nodded.

"That is to be the main crematorium—one building as large as the entirety of the camp you're in now. Cognac?" Heinrich extended a brandy snifter toward his son.

"No, thank you, father."

The elder Engel left his study and made his way to the sitting room, leaving Karl to marvel at what he saw.

Moments later, Karl followed his father, entering the sitting room where he saw all the recent photos of his father posing with all the right people of the Party, minus one.

"Everyone, but the Fuhrer, himself. But, that's right around the corner." He sat in his brown leather chair. "Now, your news, then, if you please."

Mrs. Engel sat in her chair, hands neatly folded in her lap.

"I'm being given a commendation."

Karl's father nearly knocked his chair over, jumping up with excitement. "Excellent! Our son, the rising Nazi! I'm sure a promotion is right around the corner. I knew you had it in you. I told you," he said, turning to his wife, "the military was the way for him to rise in the Party. Just wait until we win the war. We'll be dining with the Fuhrer by Christmas, and then my photo collection will be complete! To what do we owe this great honor?"

"I killed a Jew—practically with my bare hands."

"Fantastic, son!" Heinrich threw his arm around Karl's shoulders, gesturing toward a wall, as if a Jew's head hung there like a prized stag's. "You've killed your first Jew. My son is a man. You know, this is no different than when one is no longer a virgin."

"Thank you, father." Karl felt his cheeks redden. "That's not the only reason I'm here, though."

"Go on."

"I have a question for mother."

"Yes, Karl?" Olga asked in a soft, demure voice.

"I have a friend at work whose wife recently had a baby, and he was sharing details about the birth of his son. I was wondering about any details you can give me of my birth."

"What?" she asked, startled, looking to her husband.

"That is another asinine question, Karl," said his father, sitting back down, his warm, celebratory demeanor quickly growing cold. "Men do not speak of such womanly things. Your friend is filling your head with feminine ideas. Clearly, he is not someone with whom you should continue to associate. It is a shame if that is truly one of the reasons you came all this way. No, we will change the subject immediately. Now, tell me, son, what's it like being around so many...Jews." Even the taste of the word appeared to foul his mouth.

"Lately, it's becoming more difficult to...differentiate, that they're Jewish, just by appearance."

"That's because they all look alike. Of course, it's difficult to tell one from another."

"No, I mean, difficult to tell Jew from non-Jew."

Karl's father scoffed. "Nonsense. I've never heard of such a thing. I have no problem distinguishing a Jew from a person—they're not people!"

"That's not all. It's becoming increasingly difficult when Jew babies and children come into my workplace. All the Jews that come in there have fear in their eyes, but the fear in the young ones' eyes is different; it's as if they know what's about to happen to them, and they're asking me 'why?' That's what I see in their eyes." Karl noted his father's look of disgust at his son's sentimentality. "Mother, father, how would you handle being near a Jew baby?"

"I wouldn't go near the thing," his mother said, displaying her own thought and feelings for the first time during the visit.

The Camp

"The young Jews are not asking you a damn thing," began Heinrich. "Just like their elders, they have no thought process. I know what goes on in the camps, and I say keep sending them there, no matter their age. A weed does not become a rose as it matures. It's best to clear the garden of such intrusive things, before they take over and stifle the true beauty within. The best time to do that is before the weeds get too big."

Mister Engel leaned back in his chair, shaking his head, as he continued. "I don't understand. You come with such joyous news, then tell us all these things that you find…difficult." He sipped his Cognac. "You're beginning to disrupt my happiness, Karl."

"That is not my intention, father. I simply want to be the best Nazi possible, and be more like you. Please, tell me again why you hate the Jews so much."

"I appreciate that, Karl," Heinrich said, a strange, off-putting smile creeping up. "I will be more than happy to help. They are a usurious plague that festers and feeds upon the wealth and humanity of an unwitting populace. They caused us to lose the first war, sending your beloved country into the deep depression of Weimar from which only our great Fuhrer has been able to dislodge us.

"Be thankful that I sent you to the Nazi Party Youth Headquarters in Berlin, helping you to get your foot in the door of where you are now. Well, that and some strings I had to pull to get you into one of the camps I worked on." The elder man shook his head. "I'm thankful the party was able to get rid of that God-awful Bauhaus movement that was in that Berlin building, though."

"Father, please, you were saying?"

"Yes. Well, Hitler saved us, and that saving requires a sacrifice, an offering—of those responsible for our dear Fatherland's near-demise. We must do everything possible to aid our Fuhrer. His struggle has been every pure German's struggle, and now, he needs our help, and we must give it to him."

"I see," said Karl.

"Do you? I'm not sure, at the moment." The imposing man set his snifter on the glass coffee table. "You have done well in receiving your commendation, and in killing your first Jew by hand, yet you seem on the fence about the purity of your work. So, let me help remedy that."

Heinrich burst from his chair, sending his Cognac flying, the amber liquor splashing on Olga's yellow dress as she sat trembling. He grabbed his son by the throat, squeezing hard. "What commandment have I always taught you to value above all others?"

"Honor thy father," whispered Karl, straining.

"Heinrich, please," Olga pleaded, rising from her chair.

The young Nazi's father turned to her, without saying a word. Karl knew the man needed to supply only a single glare. Olga slowly sat back in her seat.

"Right," said the older Nazi, slowly turning his head back around to Karl. "Bringing honor to your father, and honoring what he commands, is what matters most. Right now, you have two fathers: me, and he who sits in Berlin, leading us to glory. Now, I don't know what kind of game you're playing, telling us about a commendation, then talking such nonsense and wasting my time, but I will not play your game.

"You've always been weak, Karl. You were a sick baby, a weak child, until your pure blood kicked in and cleansed you of any impurities you may have had, but weak you have remained. Now, you have the opportunity to raise yourself above what you've always been. You are a member of a pure race, and you need to act like it. I've gone to great lengths to create…to bring up the perfect family that would help me…help us rise in the party. And, all this talk is undermining that. So you return to your work today, and question these things no more. You are SS-Totenkopfverbande—act like it! Do you understand?"

Karl nodded as best he could.

"Very well," said his father, releasing Karl to fall on the floor. "Now that our discussion is over, I have work to do. As do you. Your mother will see you out."

CHAPTER TWELVE

Hours later, with night fallen, Karl sat in the Kubelwagen, parked somewhere off-road, in the dark woods that surrounded the majority of the camp's perimeter. He'd returned to his worksite, but not because his father had told him to. In truth, Karl never had any intention of going to Berlin. He simply needed more than one day off to process his life's recent turn-of-events.

He had requested a second day off for this very reason—to get drunk, alone, outside the camp. No distractions, no interruptions, just time to himself to try to get a handle on all of the different emotions that were swallowing him whole. To watch, and think about, from an outsider's vantage point, the place that had become his entire world, and where his entire world had been turned upside down. His unwitting co-conspirator in an act of larceny was his mother who, thanks to a fortuitous distraction from her husband, had allowed her son to swipe his father's Cognac. The slender bottle of Armagnac Ryst Dupeyron brandy, vintage nineteen thirty-nine, now rested safely, warmly, in Karl's hand.

The camp, the place where his past, present, and future had all collided in one chance meeting, one night, one moment when he heard that Miriam was his real mother. This prison that had become the link between the ideas that had shaped him and what he held to be absolute truths, and the revelation that everything he knew was a lie.

They don't even know, he thought. *My parents don't even know I'm Jewish. You're supposed to be able to tell just by looking at them, and a Jew lived right under them without ever being suspected. All those telling features they're supposed to have, and I have none. My parents—that word is so funny, now.* Karl laughed to himself.

Create the perfect family? Help him rise in the party?

There are certain moments that seem to be tailor-made for liquor. At this moment, to Karl, no liquor he'd had before had ever tasted so good.

What the hell did he mean when he said he'd created the perfect family? Then the fucker slipped up again, saying I was a sick baby, a weak child.

Karl recounted the conversation with his adoptive mother, Olga, as she saw him out of the house.

"What does father mean, I was a sick baby?"

"A lot of babies are born sick, dear," said Olga, straightening her son's collar. "You were no different, but you grew up to be strong. I'm very proud of the man you are today. Don't worry about your father—he works so hard, and we really shouldn't be so burdensome on him with any silliness. Everything he does, and everything you do now, can only work in our favor to make us more prominent citizens in the new Deutschland."

"Yeah, I'm not too concerned with him, or Germany, at this moment. Let's get back to me being a sick baby, and a weak child."

"It was nothing. No one really knows. You were late in walking, you had trouble moving your arms, some difficulty breathing at times, things like that. There were times when I—we—thought we were going to lose you. It was so long ago, I don't even remember what the doctors said that you may have had. You were always a very good boy, though, always did what you were told, but you didn't really gain any strength until you were about five-years-old."

"Where was father during all of that?"

"He…worked a lot," she said, appearing distant, but suddenly snapping back. "Listen to me. You were an ill child, but God saved you for something great, and your father and I are witnessing that greatness today. You've killed your first Jew, like a brave knight protecting the Fatherland from intruders, or going off on a Crusade. I love you very much, Karl. Always remember—family comes first."

Family comes first. The new Germany. Feeling the sudden urge to empty his alcohol-soaked bladder, Karl got out of the Kubelwagen, walked to the front driver-side of the vehicle, and urinated on the tiny Nazi flag, laughing.

He climbed onto the spare tire and sat down, refocusing his thoughts, clearing his mind of his German parents. He took a long drink.

What's she doing right now? he wondered, his thoughts turning to Else. He looked at his watch—ten o'clock. *Should be sleeping. Is she? Can she sleep in there? Idiot, why do you care? You're no one to her, except the guy who tried to rape her.*

A bigger drink.

The Camp

They stand on two legs, and breathe oxygen. They speak German like us. All body parts are in the right places. Their skin feels the same, looks the same. They eat and drink. They love and fear, bleed and die. They bleed and die. The idea that they are not human has no logic.

A longer drink. Karl ran the bottle along his forehead.

All this hatred; all this death.

He stared at the camp through the bottle..

But, I didn't rape her. I didn't hurt her.

Karl got off the car's hood, and paced.

I have a brother, and a sister. My mom's name is Miriam, not Olga, but Miriam. And my father. I killed my father.

He ran his fingers through his dark hair, pulling at it, shutting his eyes tight. Putting the bottle's neck to his lips, he took the longest drink yet.

My family are prisoners, sentenced to die by their presence, their presence dictated by them being different. She's going to die. None of this makes any damn sense.

I'm Jewish. I'm Jewish, and I'm out here, while they're in there. I would be in there, a prisoner, with them, if she hadn't given me up. If my father hadn't adopted me. My Jew hating, Nazi father.

But, I am a prisoner—a prisoner of my birth and my upbringing. No one can know. I can't save them. I can't protect them. I can't help them.

I can't save her. What the fuck do I do?

Karl finished the Cognac, throwing the empty bottle into the woods. Stumbling to the driver's side, he got in the car, and sat, staring at the searchlights of the camp.

What the fuck do I do?

He leaned his head back on the headrest, and passed out.

CHAPTER THIRTEEN

Finally returning to duty at the camp, having spent his second day off in the car in the woods, recuperating and so preoccupied by his thoughts and his situation that he was unable to go anywhere else, the first place he headed to was 'A' Barracks, on the men's side of the camp—Albert Fogel's residence.

The interior of the building looked exactly the same as the women's, multiple rows of wooden bunks, three bunks to a stack, each bed providing accommodations for three prisoners. Closer to the door than Miriam's bed was, he found Albert's bunk, the bottom one, with one of the current residents occupying it at that very moment. Karl knew that, though; he knew that Albert had been bedridden, convalescing, since the beating. As he drew near, Karl saw his double sleeping. Albert was alone in the barracks when Karl stopped beside the bed.

The Nazi stood there, intrigued, watching the wounded weave in and out of whatever terrible dream he was having. Karl figured that, whatever the man's subconscious mind was creating, he was probably the antagonist of the scene being played out. And, there was a part of Karl that enjoyed it, having that kind of effect, on this Jew that lay before him, but then, something else emerged from within, something unexpected and for the most part, unusual, given his typical thought process regarding his work. He wasn't sure how to react to this new emotion—guilt.

He wondered if he should just go ahead and put the man out of his misery, right here, right now. One bullet to the head—quick, easy, painless. It would be a greater death, a more merciful one, than most other Jews who enter the place get. He knew there would be no questions asked; everyone was expecting it, anyway.

Albert had, in fact, already been scheduled to be taken out back and shot, like a diseased dog, until Karl, at the last moment, requested otherwise. No one had asked why Karl stopped the execution; he was making a name for himself for his cruelty—even among the SS. The young Nazi was being given a lot of leg room to stretch as he saw fit. His father had gotten him in, gotten him a cushy assignment, away from any fighting, but it was Karl himself who was creating his own reputation.

Karl, still standing there, pondering what to do, watched Albert's bruised, near-rainbow-colored eyes unfurl slowly, close again as if shut by an invisible hand, then flip half-open again, like a broken shade, the terror in them so evident. It was clear that Albert was aware that he was no longer dreaming.

Karl's brother had the same fear and trembling shakes that Else had produced when the Nazi had visited Miriam, and he noticed the middle area of the top sheet, right around Albert's waist area, grow wet.

"Relax," Karl said. "I'm not here to kill you."

Albert continued shaking, as the wet spot spread, clinging to the body underneath. The internal and external pain of his injuries flooded his face with each convulsion.

"How are you feeling?" asked Karl.

The man's eyes widened as he drew the sheet closer to his face, as if trying to further conceal himself from the gray monster that had crept out of his bedroom closet, and now stood at the foot of his bed, pausing only momentarily before devouring its meal.

"Hmm, I do understand your trepidation in answering," the Nazi said. "My name is Karl, and I know who your mother is; don't worry, she's unharmed. As is your sister, Sarah." Karl paced back and forth along the bunk. "But, I have spoken with her, Miriam that is, and I've learned a great many things. Things that, over the past couple of days, after much reflection, I have come to, regretfully, believe. I assure you, it was not easy to come to this conclusion, but after examining various factors in my life, not the least of which being that I look nothing like my parents, the ones that raised me, it seems that the unfortunate fact remains: you and I are brothers."

Karl stopped pacing, looking down on Albert's face, into his own reflection. Now he knew what the horror in his own face looked like to Miriam two days earlier.

"Yes, well, as I said," Karl continued, pacing again, "it is a regretful conclusion. We are twins, Miriam is my mother, and Sarah is my sister. And, Jakob, your father…"

"Is dead, isn't he?" Albert whispered, his mouth noticeably dry.

Karl stopped, his back to Albert. "Yes." What seemed like an eternity passed before Karl spoke again. "I did not know. And, even if I had, there would have been nothing that I could have done. Given his condition, he was unable to work. If you were anyone else, you'd be dead now, too, given your injuries which make you of little use. I have, for the moment, supplied you with a temporary stay of execution. You must understand, however, that no one can know who you truly are to me. No one can find out that we are connected by birth."

"That you are Je—."

"Careful." Karl whipped around. "Do not feel so comfortable with me that you can say whatever you like." Karl sat on the bottom bunk across from Albert. "But, I did come here to discuss matters with you. I will keep you alive, as long as you are useful, though, like I said, this must be kept secret. You have no idea to what length they will go to determine the *facts* of this case, medically speaking."

Albert's lost expression exasperated Karl.

"We are twins," the guard continued. "If they found out that you were a twin, you would beg for the chamber. And your begging would fall on deaf ears. So would mine."

"May I ask a question?" asked Albert.

"You may speak."

"Why do you hate us so much? What have we done to you?"

Karl hung his head toward the floor. "You cannot expect to receive, or even understand, the answer to a question like that in the few minutes that I have. Obviously, my life has taken a different path, one which you will never understand. My father…" Karl paused, ruminating on his choice of phrasing, before he continued. "Look, this is how I've grown up. It's what I've been taught, from the very beginning. You also cannot expect to suddenly switch all of that off. No matter what our connection is, when I look at you, of course, I see myself, but I also see all the filth that has tried to contaminate the Fatherland. And, seeing both of those at the same time really plays with a person's mind. You people have done nothing but assimilate the indigenous people of a country into your plan for world domination.

"But, now, there's you, Albert. I am fully aware that I was given up for medical reasons, but what if it had been you that were given up? Do you believe that you would be the person you are today? You would be no different than I am, if it had been you that had been raised by the same people who raised me. A sailboat will be driven in the very direction in which the wind behind it blows, regardless of the hands that built it. It will not diverge."

"Do you like what you do?" Albert asked.

"Perhaps."

"There is no part of your job, your life, that you do not like?"

Karl thought for a moment. "Though I know what they grow up to be, I admit that I don't enjoy what becomes of the children who come here."

"I have not seen any--."

Karl snapped his eyes in Albert's direction, locking onto his twin's glassy stare.

"Oh," said Albert. "So you are human."

"Careful—it's a thin line between courageous and stupid. What is your point in asking me if I like any of it?"

"I think there is a part of you that knows all of this is wrong."

"You sound like your mother," Karl said, standing. "The only part of me that matters is the pure part. We are the ubermensch of which Nietzsche speaks. Even the Americans, with their Superman, ascribe to this idea, the superior race. I am part of that, no matter where I began, or who built me, that is the river upon which I now flow. And, you do not."

"I've read Superman—created by two Jews."

Karl stared at his brother, his twin, lying beaten in his bed, the wet sheet sticking to his worn body. Suddenly, he saw himself lying in the bunk, bruised and bloodied. "Yes, well, when you are well enough, I have secured a new job for you, one that may prolong your life for a time, which will nonetheless end eventually, as there is nothing I can truly do for you."

"Thank you, Karl."

"Do not address me as your equal. I am your superior, in all aspects. You must not speak my name again. And, do not thank me, yet. You may wish that you were still cleaning latrines."

Karl stood for a moment, considering whether to ask the next question on his mind, until he finally decided. "Do you know Else?"

"Yes, I know her. Why do you ask?"

"Nothing."

Karl began to walk away, when he suddenly stopped. "I'll send a new blanket to you, and some food and water. You need to get better as quickly as possible to begin your new assignment."

Karl exited the barracks, leaving Albert alone to continue mending.

CHAPTER FOURTEEN

A week had passed since their conversation, and Karl now led Albert toward the exit of the latter's barracks. The early March sun tried vainly to break through late-winter's colorless sky, an icy chill enveloping the two as they stepped outside amid a heavy snowfall. Karl had to check twice to make sure it really was snow, and not ash. Still, even the white accumulating on the frozen, brown, muddy ground couldn't keep gray from being the dominant color of their environment.

"Where are we going?" Albert asked, shivering in his two-sizes-too-big striped outfit that hung loosely around his thinning frame. "It's so cold."

Some of the external signs of Karl's attack had healed, though it was obvious from the prisoner's slow movements that the internal wounds persisted. It didn't help that Albert had lost about twenty pounds in the week and a half since he arrived at the camp.

"It's best that you don't ask too many questions," said Karl. "The little that you know about what goes on around here, including whatever I do, the better off you are."

"I didn't think I was going to see you again, since you hadn't come back."

"I'm trying not to draw suspicion toward us," the guard whispered. "Just keep looking down. If anyone speaks, don't look up, and definitely don't make eye contact. Now, hush."

Karl looked around as he pushed Albert along, crunching their way through the snow, Karl in his shiny black boots, and Albert in his thin, worn, brown shoes, with the former turning his head from side to side, checking from time to time, to see if they were drawing any attention. Karl covered his ears periodically, shielding them from the cold.

Prisoners continued their work, like any other day: on construction sites, cleaning latrines, running errands for the SS, and anything else that kept them busy and moved them closer to death. Hammers fell a little less vigorously in the cold, but fall they did. The guards were dressed warmly in their long, gray coats, and black gloves; the Kapos were covered slightly better than the other inmates. Smoke from the furnaces continued rising, like it always did, day and night, swirling into the driving wind of the gray sky.

The pair made their way past the latrines, the rows and rows of barracks, the guard towers, and the bodies. No one was bothering to pick up the fallen, frozen bodies strewn across the camp, the black stripes of the outfits being the only signs that there was any kind of obstruction on the ground. Not that this visual-aid always helped, as Karl watched another guard nearly fall, tripping over one of the cadavers, then pull out his pistol, fire two shots into the icy flesh of the dead, and continue walking, cursing under the mist of his escaping breath. The cold kept any rotting odor at bay.

Finally, after what seemed like an hour's walk in the thickening snowfall, though it had really only taken several minutes, they arrived at a spot in the fence, no too far away, but neither too close to the general population.

"Okay," Karl said, "you can look up now."

Standing on the other side of the fence, separated by a couple of yards, and yet another fence, were Miriam, Sarah, and Else, all huddled together. Each row of fencing was topped with barbed wire.

Nervous, Karl scanned the surrounding area again, searching for any curious eyes. *So far, so good*, he thought.

"Okay, everybody," said the Nazi, observing everyone around him trembling from the cold, "make it as quick as possible. It's freezing out here, but there really was no better time to do this. And, remember—no big movements or gestures. Don't look overly emotional."

Even through the white veil, he saw tears flow easy down everyone's cheeks.

"You okay?" Miriam asked, her hands raised slightly in Albert's direction.

Karl was keen to her desire to embrace her son, worrying that others may notice, as well.

"Yes," said Albert. "Getting better. I miss you."

"Be careful what you say," said Karl in a low voice, but making sure the whole family could hear. "I told you, try not to say anything that may elicit any kind of strong emotional reaction. Don't attract attention. You people are not the only ones on the line, here."

"Is everything alright where you are?" Miriam continued, turning her gaze from Karl back to Albert.

"Yes. Everything is okay."

"He is fine, for now," said Karl. "That's the best I can offer. I'm going to do what I can, but I have no control over your fates. I'm risking a lot as it is, right now."

"I know, son. Thank you."

Karl looked at Else. "Are you okay?"

She looked away from Albert, furrowed her brow at Karl, and turned again toward the imprisoned brother.

"Hey, Sarah," said Albert. "You're still as beautiful as ever."

Sarah, looking a couple of years younger with her thinning frame, wept a little harder. "You never called me beautiful before."

"I never said a lot of things before that I should have."

Karl watched Albert's attention move to Else. She cast her gaze down, a sad smile following.

"Me, too," Else mouthed.

Karl looked down at his feet, trying to ignore any and all feelings that started creeping up inside. It was all still so alien to him, these emotions for a Jew. Instead, he tried to focus on how cold he was, and how warm he would be once the meeting was over and he got Albert back to his barracks.

"Is dad over there with you?" the sister continued. "Mom keeps saying she doesn't know."

"I think he's around here somewhere," stammered Albert, his teeth chattering.

Karl saw that his brother began to break. He looked around and noticed, through the white shroud, Wilhelm, Hans, and Klaus watching from a distance, all three smoking cigarettes.

"Okay," he said. "That's it. Time's up. We gotta go. We're being watched, and you're all going to freeze to death, which will have completely wasted my time and energy with what I'm going to do."

Karl grabbed Albert by the arm.

"Everyone pay close attention for just a few seconds longer, though. I need all of you prepared to move tomorrow. Say nothing to anyone. Just be ready to go quickly when I come."

Out of the corner of his eye, Karl saw his three friends still looking in his direction.

"We gotta go, Albert. Play along."

Karl motioned with his head for the women to move away from the fence, and go find something to do, then gave his brother a rough jerk, nearly throwing him to the ground. As his prisoner regained his balance, Karl pushed him hard, quickening his pace back to the barracks.

CHAPTER FIFTEEN

It was early the next morning when Karl ventured over to the female side of the camp. He walked like a gray blot, and felt even more so, across the still white, snow-covered terrain. The accumulation from the previous day had reached a couple of inches.

He'd noticed that, because of the conflux of all the death that surrounded him and the recent familial discovery, he was beginning to lose all internal feeling, much like, he imagined, what someone with a missing limb must feel. Unless, he also discovered, he was thinking of Else, though even that he tried to mask, even to himself.

Searching the women's side in the cold light of dawn, he finally found Miriam, Else, and Sarah hard at work. The three, like the many other women around them, sat at long tables, out in the cold, making socks for the German troops out of the hair that had been shorn from the living. Two women lay on the red and white ground, their blood mixed with the snow. They'd fallen backward from where they sat as they were working, after being been shot in the forehead from the opposite side of the table.

"Let's go," he said to Miriam, tugging at her arm.

"Right now? Won't I get in trouble for getting up now?"

"When one of us approaches you, just do as you're told, when you're told to do it. Especially, if it's me."

Karl looked at Else, and Sarah, nodding with his head that it was time to stand and follow him.

"I'm going to tell you the same things I told Albert," he said with a stern look, pointing his finger in all their faces, as if they were being lectured for a misdeed, to keep any other guards from suspecting anything. "Keep looking down, don't make eye contact, don't draw attention, don't ask questions, and do *exactly* as I say."

He led the three to the gate keepers of the women's side, handing papers to the guards on post.

"They're going *there*?" asked one of the men. "Why weren't they put there before? Their heads are already shaved."

"An oversight on someone's part," said Karl. "Look, they're from Theresienstadt. Hey, I just do as I'm told; do you want to be the one who doesn't?"

The guard looked at the women, then back down at the papers. "Very well," he said.

"Let's go, Jew witches," Karl said, pushing his mother. "Now, all of you listen carefully," he whispered, clearing the gate, "while we've got a few minutes to walk for me to tell you what's going on. You're being moved to what's called 'family camp.' It's very new and they could decide to get rid of it at any time, but it's better than where you are now. Else, you'll have to pretend to be Miriam's other daughter, Sarah's older sister.

"All of you will be able to grow your hair back out, and you'll write letters to people you know on the outside, telling them that this place isn't that bad, to dispel any rumors they've heard about what goes on here. Like I said, they just decided to do this, so it's not quite finished, but you'll find men, women, and children living where you're going. And, before you ask, no, Albert will not be joining you. People were watching us yesterday, and it would look too suspicious if I moved all of you to family camp. No one can know he's your son, or that I'm his brother. He has to be kept separated. I've arranged a job for him; it's not good, but it will buy him some more time. That's the best I can do."

As the group trudged toward a new side of the camp, Karl spied Hans nearing them.

"Hey, Karl," began Hans, "what's going on?"

Karl noted nothing sinister in the question. "Not much. Just transferring some prisoners."

"Me, Klaus, and Wilhelm saw you yesterday talking to some Jews by the fence."

Still, nothing to really worry about. "Yeah, I had noticed them talking to each other through the fence before, and since I was still in a good mood from the commendation, I decided to give them all a warning."

Suddenly, Karl saw Hans' eyes focus on a particular prisoner.

"Hey, isn't that the girl from--."

"Yes," Karl said, trying to think quickly, knowing this moment would likely get back to Klaus. "I've decided to move her so she wouldn't be able to cast any more hexes on me—or anyone else. I'm trying to keep my friends safe."

"Good idea, Karl. I wish I could get as far away from all these Jews as possible. I'll let you keep going. Talk to you later, my friend."

"Sure."

"Is everything okay?" asked Miriam, continuing the walk.

"Fine," said Karl.

Approaching the entry point to family camp, Karl gave the three women a few final instructions. "I'll check on you every few days. Just like where you were before, do as you're told. Now, keep your heads down."

Karl handed the papers to the guard at the new gate, who looked at the women, and furrowed his brow.

"Whatever," said the man, practically tossing the papers back to Karl. "Go in, go to work."

Karl waited a moment for them to enter, only to see that they were too scared to move. "Go, Jews!"

Finally, they entered and, leaving Miriam, Sarah, and Else in their new home, Karl walked back to the men's side of the camp, and retrieved Albert.

"But, where am I going?" whispered Albert. "What's the job?"

"Shut up, damnit. Listen, as much as you will wish I hadn't told you, I'm *about* to tell you, on our way there."

Karl shoved Albert ahead of him, guiding the prisoner by his arm, as they took their long walk.

"You see those smoke stacks up ahead?" asked Karl. "That's where you're going."

"But, isn't that...?" Albert began. "You said I had a new job. I don't understand."

"I also said to shut up," said Karl, almost growling. "You do have a new job. No one is going to kill you. Not today. Not as long as you do as you're told.

"You will be what's called a Sonnderkommando. You will work in the gas chambers. Your job is to remove the bodies from the chamber, get them to the ovens, and then clean the showers for the next group."

"What?" Albert began to squirm, causing Karl to tighten his grip, and jerk him back.

"Do you want to live or die?" Karl asked. "You could die in an hour if you stayed where you were; here, you are needed, you have a purpose, so they're less likely to get rid of you. At least, for a while."

"I'd rather die."

"Don't be stupid. Look, I know it's hard, I know what you're being asked to do. Especially, since you're not completely healed, yet, and it will be difficult for you to keep up the pace with the other Sonderkommando. But, you must keep up with them, or you will no longer be useful, and you'll get what you want—they will kill you. That's why there's an opening for the job, now. And, you're getting it."

As before, when the pair reached the guard at the crematorium, Karl handed over Albert's transfer papers. This time, the guard didn't even look at them, just motioned for the new Sonderkommando to go in.

Karl had always tried to avoid this particular set of barracks as much as possible. The housing smelled of death, not the dead, not corpses, but of death itself, occupied by the living dead, the Sonderkommando, those skeletal minions of the Grim Reaper, with their sunken, lifeless eyes, and sallow skin. This was the home of those poor souls who escorted others to their end, but who were forced to wait to find their own finality, unless they found it by way of their own frail fingers.

Karl released his firm grip on Albert's arm, and pushed him forward. Turning around, to head back to his own post, Karl found Klaus, Wilhelm, and Hans standing behind him.

"What are you doing?" Klaus asked. "Isn't that the Jew that's supposed to look like you, but you don't think he does?"

"That's him," said Karl, feeling the pressure to think quickly, his heart racing, afraid they could see his chest pulsating. Hans confronting him was one thing, Klaus, on the other hand, was entirely different.

"He's the one you were beating several days back, too, right?"

"Yeah," said Wilhelm, "and we saw you with him down by the fence, yesterday."

"What's going on?" asked Klaus. "Why are you moving him here? Why are you even keeping him alive? Why don't you just kill him, like you were obviously going to do? Plus, Hans said he saw you earlier moving three women, one of them being the girl from the shower."

"Really? Hans told you that, huh?" Karl didn't bother glaring at Hans for talking. He knew Klaus' crony would talk, but that's all he was doing—talking. Neither Hans, nor Wilhelm, had the forethought to conspire.

"I just want to make sure that you are careful about what you're doing," said Klaus. "There are a lot of people around who could get the wrong idea about things."

"Yes, there are people who have no business asking me what I do. You're right."

Karl and Klaus stared at each other for several seconds, seemingly sizing up each other's next move in their game of verbal chess.

"Anyway," Karl continued, "I've decided that he would be someone I could have fun with." He did his best to deflect any attention away from Else.

His three friends gave him curious looks.

"Like a pet," said Klaus.

"Yes, exactly," Karl followed. "Like a pet. Now, like a dog fetching sticks, I have him fetching dead Jews."

His friends laughed, as did he. He felt relieved.

"You know," began Wilhelm, "I've heard of people having pets that looked like them. You know, people who look like their dogs."

"Yeah," said Hans, "my mother had a schnauzer once. I didn't know which one I needed to walk at night."

The four friends laughed together as they walked back to their posts, ready to receive the next batch of incoming Jews.

CHAPTER SIXTEEN

A few nights later, Karl, heavily intoxicated, entered the side of the concentration complex known as family camp. The temperature had risen slightly in the last few days, to melt some snow, but it was really comparable to peeling back only the top-most layer of an onion. The first thing he noticed was the lack of frozen bodies lying on the ground. The illusion that the Nazis were hoping for when family camp was created, that it was not *that* bad in the camp, was coming to fruition.

Passing through several barracks housing a few small groups each of men, women, and children, he searched the buildings looking for her. The housing in family camp smelled a little better than they had on the other side of the camp, but not by much. All the bunks were different here than the former residence from where Karl had brought the women, the new side having the normal two beds per stack, sleeping one to two prisoners on each bed, allowing for a little more room.

The women did, indeed, wear dresses, like they could in Kanada, another partition of the camp where women were better treated. Karl had chosen family camp over Kanada, however, because he figured it was going to be an easier sell with their heads already shaven. Plus, Kanada had a reputation of allowing the better looking female prisoners in, quite often for sexual purposes, whether the women wanted it or not.

Then there were the children. Karl found kids of all ages living in family camp, though not many at this point, since the implementation of the idea was still in its own infancy. Some of the children Karl came across kept themselves busy playing games; the most common he saw during his quick trek through the barracks, searching for Else, was hide-and-seek. Sometimes, when the parents weren't paying attention, the children doing the seeking pretended to be Nazis.

Finally, in one of the last barracks, he found Else, in a white dress, sitting on a bunk, writing a letter. She startled and gasped when she looked up, and saw Karl standing there.

"I'm sorry," he said to Else, smiling bigger than he intended. "I didn't mean to scare you."

He heard the slight, quickened creaking of the wood bunk as she trembled. Karl watched her look around, on her other side, and grab another female, pulling her closer.

"Who's your letter to?" he asked.

"Else," said the woman held so tightly by Karl's object of affection, "you're hurting me."

"No one," Else said, in a soft voice, her reddening, welling eyes staring at Karl.

"No one?" he asked. He kept smiling. "Then where do your letters go? Where's your family?"

"They're dead," said Else. "They died in the ghetto." She looked around. "Miriam and Sarah are over there, somewhere." She pointed toward another corner of the barracks.

Karl fidgeted with Else's blanket, if one could call the thin sheet she used to keep warm at night, a blanket. That part hadn't changed during the move from one side of the camp to the other.

"Yeah, I saw them over there. I'm not here to see them." He worked hard to control his facial muscles, hoping he was conveying the right expression. He nervously folded his arms in front of him, dropped them to his sides, then folded them again. "I'm sorry about your family."

Else didn't speak, only continuing to cling tight to the white dress sleeve of the other prisoner.

"This is the first time we've had a chance to talk since the other night, when we first met," Karl continued. "I wanted to see how well you're doing."

Karl felt a tiny tug on his gray pants. He looked down to see a girl with dark hair and brown eyes, about five-years-old, standing beside him.

"Yes?" he asked, perturbed that he was being interrupted when finally able to get a moment with Else.

"Herr soldier," she began, "have you seen my daddy? I saw him outside, but now I can't find him in here."

"Well, if you saw him outside earlier, then he's probably with the other men, or daddies, in a different building." He turned his attention back to Else.

"This is our first day here," continued the little girl. "Do you think my daddy is safe? Are me, my mommy, and my sister, safe now?"

Karl's mind left the scene for a moment, drifting across the camp to the incoming trains and the crematoria. He pictured the children being sent to the left, and heard the screams from the showers.

"Safe?" he asked, bending down to the little girl, the alcohol coursing through his body, fueling his rapid unhinging. "You want to know if you, and your family, are safe?"

The girl nodded, but Karl only rose back up, leaving her question unanswered. He looked at Else, watching her shake, as the tears she'd been able to dam up finally broke free.

"You're crying," he said. Karl began to reach up to her cheeks, when she suddenly jolted. He pulled his hand back, and noticed her looking at the gun holstered to his side. "Hey, you want to see it? Hold it?"

Karl, inebriated, clumsily removed his weapon, turning it around in his hands to show Else the gun from every angle. Everyone in the general vicinity gasped and quietly backed away. Else had nowhere to go.

"What's going on?" asked Miriam, coming up from behind Karl, with Sarah trailing her. "Is everything okay?"

"Nothing," said Karl, trying to hide his gun behind his back. "Everything's fine." He looked back at Else. "Well, I can see you're busy. I just wanted to see you, to check on you. I'll come back later."

Sarah climbed onto the top bunk, and sat next to Else, wrapping her arms around her. The young teenager laid her shaven head against Else's back.

"Elizabeth," Miriam said to the woman standing next to Else, "you can go now. I have her."

Miriam pulled Karl aside. "What are you doing? I saw what was in your hand. Why do you have your gun out, in here? Put that away, there's kids around." She stood close to him, helping his drunken hand holster his pistol. "You reek of liquor. I don't think that now, in your condition, is a good time for you to be talking to Else. Remember the last time you were drunk around her? All of us appreciate what you have done to help. It's better here than where we were, as much as it can be, but you have to be more sensitive to various situations than you are."

"I just wanted to talk. That's all," Karl pouted.

"I know. I know you don't mean any harm. I can see that you're trying to make some changes in yourself."

"I talked to my parents." Karl paused, laughing quietly to himself. "I mean, I talked to my adoptive Nazis, and was only handed more lies."

"Listen to me, son." Miriam scanned the barracks before putting her hands on his face. "Your father, your real father, would be very proud of you. I was there that night. I remember that you sent him to the right, at first, and the doctor came back and sent him to the left. You are not to blame. Please, try to control your drinking. Come back later, when you're sober.

"And, when you do come back, keep in mind that what you did when you first met Else was very traumatic for her. I can also tell you that, she and Sarah, are very leery of you, especially after what happened with Albert, and the other man. You have to understand that this is not a normal situation. We are all suffering here. None of us know how long we have left."

"Yeah, I know she likes Albert," said Karl.

Miriam gave him a perplexed look. "I wasn't even talking about that. What does that have to do with anything? Why do you care so much about her?"

"I don't," he said, stumbling toward the door, annoyed. "Else, I'll tell your boyfriend you said, 'hi.'"

Karl, pulling a flask out of his uniform pants pocket, tripped his way out of the barracks, through the mud, and out of family camp.

CHAPTER SEVENTEEN

The next day, once his shift had ended, Karl stepped again into the family camp barracks that housed his family and Else. He had only a few minutes to speak before he had to get back to his side of the camp without arousing suspicion. Slipping quietly toward Else's bunk, he found his birth mother, and sister, sitting with the girl he couldn't get off his mind.

"May I speak to you alone?" he asked.

"It's okay, Karl," said Miriam, "you can speak in front of them."

"No. I mean can I speak in private with Else?"

Miriam and Sarah looked at each other, then at Else, seeming unsure of what to say. Else grabbed their hands.

"I don't think she wants to, Karl," Miriam said. "Maybe another time."

"Time is the most valuable thing in this place because there's so little of it. All I want to do is apologize to her." He looked at Else. "Please."

"You're sober?" Miriam asked.

"Very."

"I think you're okay," said Miriam, turning to Else. "You're safe. We'll just be a few bunks down."

Miriam got up, dragging Sarah along with her, several feet away. They stopped a few bunks down where one woman was brushing the hair of another.

Without saying a word, Karl grabbed Else by the wrist, pulled her from her bunk, and made a swift exit toward the rear door. He felt her hand try jerking away from his, but he only held tighter. Several yards away, past two other barracks, Karl led Else to the family camp's shower area.

The building was similar to the real showers on the other side of the camp, the ones without gas, with numerous shower heads hanging in evenly spaced intervals from exposed pipes above.

Karl looked outside and saw that Miriam had followed close behind.

"Karl, what are you doing?" she asked. "You were supposed to talk to her next to her bed."

"I needed a more private place. I promise she's safe. I just want to talk to her. I'll bring her back in a few minutes. Go back to your barracks, before you draw attention to us."

"You can't just do what you want like this. She's scared enough of you as it is, without you suddenly dragging her off, not knowing where she's going."

"I can do whatever I want, and I'll bring her right back. Now, go back to your barracks." Karl watched Miriam, unmoving. "I'm asking you to trust me."

Watching her finally turn around, he closed the shower area's door, and spun around to face Else. She was pale, her arms folded around her, hugging her body, trembling. Her eyes jerked around the room, over to him, then back and forth to corners. He suddenly realized that this was the first time she'd been alone with him since the attempted rape and, to make it worse, that he now had her in a shower room, again.

"I want to apologize, again, Else, for yesterday. I'm sorry I was drunk when I came to see you."

He watched her still tremble at the sight of him, at the thought of where she was and who she was with.

"And, I'm sorry for where I brought you—I wasn't thinking. I didn't mean to scare you, again. It's okay for you to talk. I want you to know that you don't have to be scared of me. I promise I'm not going to hurt you."

Else's face grew red, deepening its shade with each second that passed, as she began to transition from shock to anger.

"Did you hear me?" Karl asked, now standing only inches from her, placing his hands on her shoulders. "You don't have to be scared of me."

Else suddenly completed the transition, jolting from her coma-like state, shocking them both when she sent a hard slap across his face. Her hands flew up and covered her open mouth. Karl stepped back, saying nothing.

"I don't have to be scared of you?" she finally blurted out, continuing to seize the moment. "I am scared of you. You're a Nazi, who tried to rape me. The first time you met me, you were drunk, and you were drunk yesterday. I don't care who you're related to, or what you do for them, or me, that will never change."

"But, I didn't rape you."

"Only because you were too drunk. You think that because you *couldn't* do it, that should excuse your *attempt* to do it?"

"I admit that I've increased my drinking lately, maybe it's to deal with some things. It seems I have a taste for Cognac. Look, I'm very sorry about what happened. I didn't really want to do it. I didn't want to be a part of that. The other guys talked me into it."

"I don't care whether you really wanted to, or not. And, I don't care about your apology. You were there; you were a part of it; you tried to do it. You touched me where you shouldn't have. No man has ever touched me, except for you. No shower can wash that off. Just like my Jew smell, as you put it.

"And you saying I should accept your apology because the other guys made you do it, or something like that, is like saying you should be forgiven for what you do to all the other prisoners here, because you're just following orders. I don't think you've really changed, either. No one changes that much so quickly. I am scared of you. The only reason I'm talking to you now, is because I'm scared *not* to."

"I know I hurt you, but I'm not really violent toward women. I watched my father beat my mother when I was growing up. I moved you, and my mother and sister, to here. Is this not a better place?"

"Yes, a much softer side of hell." Her sarcasm spewed forth with her anger. "And I don't believe you're not violent. Actions speak volumes. Look at what you're a part of. I'm curious, though—why have you been taught to hate Jews all your life, anyway?"

"It's all very complicated, having to do with losing the first war, among other things. Jews are blamed for a lot. And, I was brought up as a Christian, always hearing that you people killed Jesus. Of course, that's a whole other subject I don't know *what* to do with, now."

"You people? You do realize that you're now one of us, don't you? By the way, I never killed anyone. Can you say the same?"

Karl stood silent.

"Why *did* you move us here?" she asked. "Why bring us to family camp?"

"To protect you. I'm going to protect you from now on."

She leaned back, squinting. "You can't protect us. Not really. And, you say you're not violent toward women—what about the men? What's your excuse for them? For what you did to the deaf man? To Albert, your own brother? And to Jakob, your father?"

"You don't understand," Karl huffed.

"That's the best thing you've said since you brought me here. You're right, I don't understand. Miriam talks about how she can tell that you're not the person that uniform says you are. I don't agree with her. Neither does Sarah."

Karl removed his sidearm, alarming Else, sending her back a few steps. He set the weapon on the floor, and kicked it over to her.

"You have the power, right now, Else, to do what you wish," he said.

She looked at the gun on the floor for a minute or so, the wheels in her head clearly turning, before she kicked it back to him. "I'm not like you," she said.

"And, I'm not like them, not anymore," said Karl, picking up the pistol. "Not if people will just give me a chance to change and prove it. I don't know what it means to be Jewish."

"And, I don't know what it's like to not be hated for being different. Looks like neither one of us will ever know the other's side."

Karl was desperate to change the subject.

"You knew my brother, Albert, from before the camp, right?"

"Yes."

"How do you know him?"

"We're from the same neighborhood."

"That's what my mom, I mean, Miriam, said." Karl rubbed his head. "But, how did you know him?"

"Why? So you can use some information against him? Where is he? What did you do with him? What job does he have?"

Karl grew perturbed. "Albert this, and Albert that. Were you two ever together?"

"None of these questions are any of your business. Where is he?"

"Safe, for now. He has a new job that makes him valuable. That's all I could do. Else, I need to take you back to your barracks, now. Is there something I can get for you? Anything you need that I could smuggle over?"

"Please, don't say my name. It makes my skin crawl. Just being around you, makes me nervous, and afraid. So, if you want to do something for me, please leave, and don't talk to me anymore. I really don't understand why you're talking to me; I don't know what it is you want."

"I don't, either," he whispered. "I'll go now."

"You need to spend more time with your mom and sister," she said. "You should get to know them. You can't imagine what any of us are going through."

"Would you like to see Albert?" Karl looked down at his boots.

"I don't see how it's possible, since we're on completely opposite sides of the camp, now."

"I can arrange it."

"Then, yes, I would."

"And, I *will* protect you—Else."

Karl opened the door, not giving her time to retort, and led her quickly back to the barracks.

CHAPTER EIGHTEEN

"Are you sure about this?" Albert asked, the following night.

"Yes," said Karl. "And, no."

The pair walked, the Nazi is his gray uniform, and the prisoner in his striped pajamas, as inconspicuous as possible, over what little snow still remained, from Albert's new living quarters near the crematoria, to the opposite side of the camp—to family camp. Karl smelled the dead, and the human ash, on Albert.

"What do you mean? Is it safe for us to be doing this, or not?"

"I'm a Jew, dressed like a Nazi, escorting one Jewish prisoner, who happens to be my twin, to the other end of a concentration camp so he can have a *date* with another Jewish prisoner. If you can think of any way that we can make it even *less* safe than it already is, let me know—I'll add it to the list."

"You're sure she wants to see me?"

"Do you really think I'd be taking all these risks if she *didn't* want to see you? Obviously, I'm the one that ended up with the brains."

Approaching the gate that separated family camp from the rest of the facilities, Karl reached in his pocket, and pulled out a gold tooth.

"Where did you get that?" asked Albert.

"Don't worry about it. It's your entry fee. Now be quiet."

"You people use things like that for currency?"

"You'd be surprised what goes on behind the scenes, among the guards. Now, shut up."

Karl handed the tooth to the other SS guard on post, who looked Albert up and down, then motioned with his head for the two to enter.

Karl pushed Albert farther into the camp, passing in the dark between buildings, where the former heard mothers trying to put their children to bed, to the family camp's shower area. There, past the open doors, tucked in the darkness just beyond a stream of moonlight, waited Else.

Karl watched the two nervously approach each other, her white dress, dropping past her knees, swishing as she glided across the cold cement floor. Each pair of hands drew up a few inches, wanting to reach out, only to fall back. Else let a few tears drop.

"Stay in the shadows," said Karl. "I'll close the doors a little, and be right outside."

Karl stepped out, leaving the doors cracked, and stood close enough to hear Else and Albert's conversation.

It's better this way, Karl thought. *Even if they both die in this camp, it's better that she spend her time with him. He's more like her, anyway.*

"Here," said Else, crinkling some newspaper. "Karl gave us some bread. He said this loaf is fresh, what the guards eat, not old like what we get."

"No, thanks," said Albert. "Are you guys doing okay over here? I haven't heard of this place."

"We're better here than where we were. They add a few more people each day, even children."

"Yeah, I heard some when I got over here." A few seconds of silence. "Your hair is getting longer."

Karl imagined that Albert was touching her hair, the short spikes growing longer and softer. He then imagined himself standing next to her in the shower room, running *his* fingers through her hair, her big, soft, brown eyes closing rapturously as he caressed her scalp.

"Albert, are you sure you don't want some bread? You look like you've lost a lot more weight since the last time I saw you. I mean, I know we've all gotten a little thinner in the last month, but yours looks more…extreme."

"My new job doesn't leave me with much of an appetite."

"What is your new job? Karl won't tell me."

Don't, Karl thought. *She doesn't need to know.*

"It's nothing worth hearing. I just work a lot, so I don't really have time to eat, and I've gotten used to it."

Silence permeated the large open space for several seconds, until Karl heard soft crying coming from inside. He could tell it was Albert. Then, he heard a pair of feet shuffle across the floor.

"I'm sorry," said Else. "You don't have to talk about it. The fact that we are alive and able to spend any time together in this place makes the night perfect. We don't have to talk at all if you don't want to.

"Listen," she continued. "You need to hang in there. We've got a secret radio over here, and I've heard that the Allies could be getting here soon."

Secret radio? Karl thought. He was cold outside, but kept his mind off the temperature, and on the conversation. *There's no radio. The Allies are nowhere near here. What the hell is she talking about?*

He quickly realized it was a lie, Else's fib to try to comfort Albert, to give him some hope. They were trying to protect each other from the horrors each was experiencing in the camp.

Karl wondered if she had her hand in Albert's. Were they embracing? What did that feel like? Then he noticed Albert's voice got a little lower.

"Do you like Karl? I mean, do you trust him?"

Karl waited for her to say that she was beginning to, that she could see some change in him, especially since he had brought Albert over to see her. Instead, he heard only quiet, until something soft echoed outside. Someone, in the shower room, in the dark, was whispering.

Karl, his back to the door, leaned back a little, trying to gauge the voice.

"I'm ready," said Albert, suddenly swinging the doors open. "You can take me back now."

"Are you sure?" asked Karl. "You can have a few more--."

"It's time for us to go."

"Thank you, Karl," Else said, emotionless.

"You're welcome." Karl smiled. "You'll be safe going back to your bunk, while I take Albert back to his."

Karl watched Albert start walking away, not waiting for his guard, his brother. Back into the shadows, between the barracks, they traveled.

Maybe I can stop thinking about her now, thought the Jewish Nazi. *There seemed to be a connection between them, for however long they have left.* Then it occurred to him what just ran through his mind. *She could die. Albert could die.* One word began filling his mind. *Else. Else.*

"Hey, Albert," Karl said, "I'm sorry, but this was probably the only time I could get you and Else together—at least, for a while. I think I may be drawing too much attention to you guys from some friends of mine, not to mention that if other Jews saw me bringing a prisoner from the other side of camp, just for a visit, they may try to rat you out for some special treatment for themselves. So, it's safer for all of you if I keep you apart."

"No," said Albert, "I think I know why you don't want to bring me back, and it's not for anyone's safety."

Suddenly, after crossing from the light of overhead lamps, back into the shadows, Karl felt himself pushed, not hard, into the wooden side of one of the barracks. Albert dropped to his knees. Karl quickly realized it was his brother who had, however harmlessly, attacked him.

"What the hell is wrong with you?" Karl asked. "What was that for? Are you okay?" He reached his hand out.

"Don't touch me!" snapped Albert. "You are not my brother."

"Okay, okay, I'm not your brother, just keep your voice down." Karl stood back, unsure of what to do. He knew that Albert lacked any real strength to hurt him.

"You bastard. How could you?" Albert's voice grew louder.

"I don't know what you're talking about, but you need to get quiet." Karl looked around nervously, sure that he'd heard footsteps approaching in the mud. "Stand up. We gotta get moving."

"What's going on over here?" asked a voice from behind.

Karl spun around to see another guard coming.

"This Jew talked to me," said Karl, thinking fast, "so I sent him to the ground." He looked back at Albert. "Now back on your feet, Jew! Don't make me say it twice!"

"Was he trying to escape?" asked the guard. "Where's he from?"

"No, no attempted escape. He's a Sonderkommando. He had been a good Jew, working hard at cleaning up the blood, piss, and shit from his fellow dogs, so I thought I'd reward him with a walk, like any other dog. Until he bit the hand that feeds him."

"Need any help putting him down?" The guard laughed.

"No, no. I've got a short leash waiting for him when I get him back to his kennel."

Karl pulled Albert's arm, picking him back up to his feet. "Mush, Jew."

The guard laughed again as Karl pushed Albert back toward the other side of the camp.

Finally reaching Albert's room and board, neither prisoner, nor guard, speaking the rest of the trip, Karl unlocked the door to let his brother in.

"I don't know what that was all about back there," Karl said, "but don't bother thanking me. I only did it for her, but I won't do it again. Not after what you pulled."

"Don't worry, I won't thank you. And, I'm sure she enjoyed it, just like she enjoyed what you did to her in the shower."

Albert entered his barracks, went straight to his bunk, and lay down. Karl, in shock, closed the door, locked it, and walked away.

CHAPTER NINETEEN

"And here, we have the entrance to our family camp," Karl said, strolling through the camp, chosen by his superiors to lead a tour of visiting military dignitaries.

He looked down at his formerly shiny, black boots as mud began to cake on them, replacing the snow from the previously frozen ground which was now thawing under the warmer temperatures in the past week. Karl had his uniform, like all other SS workers in the camp, neatly pressed for the visit.

Karl had previously made arrangements for the prisoners on this side of the camp to be outside, in front of the barracks, ready to be inspected by the visitors. As his group came through the gated entrance, Karl noticed the Jews were not in line as they should have been but were, instead, performing similar tasks as those prisoners in Kanada, rummaging through the suitcases, handbags, and jackets of new arrivals in an effort to plunder and pilfer any valuables which could next be sent to Berlin. Of course, Karl knew that there was some skimming going on from the SS that supervised such work, but kept it quiet so as not to attract any reprisals from those above—stealing from those who steal being one of the actual few crimes that camp workers could commit.

Children, more now residing in family camp than a week ago, were still being corralled by their mothers for inspection.

Finally, after his tour group had been waiting for far too long, according to the Standartenfuhrer's constant sighing and obvious impatience, all cleaned-up prisoners took their place in the inspection line, ready for viewing.

Karl looked down the row of Jews, nearly standing at attention, and noticed Miriam, Sarah, and Else waiting about halfway down the line. He tried not to look at Else in her pretty white dress.

Though he was speaking to the distinguished Nazis in his presence, he still had the previous week's events with Albert on his mind. Else had never left his thoughts.

I don't get it, why won't people let me move past the fucking shower? he thought, the same inner ramblings that had dogged him for a week.

"Here, they write letters to other Jews, telling them that things are not as bad as what they may have heard," Karl told the visitors.

I get them to family camp, where they have a little more freedom, where they're able to grow their hair...

"The Jew women are not required to have their heads shaven, and may wear dresses if they like."

I get Karl a job, not a desirable one, but a job that makes him of use so that he has an extension on his time...

"We even have children here, keeping some families together. It's an experiment that seems to be working."

And what do I get for all of it? Attacked. Still hated. What's the fucking point? Why do I bother? No one will let me change.

"How do you know that it works?" asked the Standartenfuhrer.

"We read each and every letter that goes out of here, sir. We make sure that they are writing what they are supposed to, but we're also making sure that no encoded correspondence leaves the camp. Plus, the Jews here seem happier, more content, thus more inclined to work, and less resistant to our rules."

I keep sticking my neck out for these people, but maybe I should just let them be, let whatever's going to happen, happen. Yeah, that's it. I'll leave them alone—no more help, no more contact. I'm finished with them.

Suddenly, something caught Karl's eye, sending his train of thought down a different set of tracks. An orange and black-spotted butterfly flew into his view, drawing his gaze beyond the prisoners, to the top of the outlying fence that formed the perimeter between the camp and a field that precipitated the surrounding forest. There, on the barbed border, the butterfly settled. Looking at the insect's bright colors in such a gray world, he realized that this was the only wildlife he'd seen since he began serving at the camp. Karl was mesmerized. The brightly colored bug quickly took flight again, rising high into the air as it suddenly dipped down toward the field and fluttered out of sight.

The Camp

Karl broke from his lack of concentration when the Standartenfuhrer in his tour group cleared his throat.

"Yes, sir," said Karl.

"I've been trying to get your attention for at least a minute. I want to know if the Jews on this side of the camp appreciate what is being done for them. Why are they more inclined to work?"

"I apologize, sir. To answer your question, yes, for the most part, they do seem to be thankful. We tend to have fewer problems in family camp, we believe, because the children are here."

"You speak as an educated young man," said the Standartenfuhrer. "You are very mature for your age. I also hear that you were chosen to conduct this tour based on your stellar performance so far in the camp. That there are even seasoned veterans who could learn a little bit from time spent in your company. And I've heard that you have a real taste for the hatred of these…Jews."

"Thank you, sir," said Karl. "Hating Jews is all I've ever known. I can't imagine what it would have been like to grow up any other way."

"Yet, I've also heard that you have calmed down in the past couple of weeks, possibly losing some of your edge."

"No, sir, not all."

"I should like very much to witness that fire in you, myself."

"Perhaps," spoke one of the camp's officers, "Engel could give you a demonstration of his Nazi prowess."

"What did you have in mind?" Karl asked.

"Well," the Standartenfuhrer began, "I do see the theoretical purpose of this family camp, but we also do not want them to become too complacent, do we? The Jews are allowed to write letters, wear dresses, keep their hair and their children, but what will be next? Will they feel that they can say, do, or even plot, whatever they want?

"If the Jews become too comfortable, our guards may follow suit, becoming too relaxed, thinking they have nothing to fear from their prisoners. No matter where they reside in the camp, fear, both within the prisoners, and within those who guard against what the prisoners may do, must be maintained at all times. Would you agree, Engel?"

"Absolutely, sir."

"Very good. I believe I will have that demonstration, now."

The Standartenfuhrer moved down the line of Jews, looking at the faces of each one, scanning their bodies. He neared the halfway mark of the line, where Karl's family, and Else, stood, proceeded a few feet past, stopped suddenly, and turned. He shot his arm out, grabbing Sarah, and jerked her into the open.

Miriam started to scream, when Karl marched quickly in front of her, making eye contact, scowling. She closed her mouth, tears falling, as other SS guards behind Karl held a writhing Sarah, trying to break free.

"Much too skinny to be of any use," said the Standartenfuhrer.

"What would you have me do, sir?" asked Karl, turning his attention to the officer.

"What we do with all useless Jews, Engel—kill her."

Karl looked back at Miriam, Else's hand covering his mother's mouth.

He walked back out in front of the dignitaries, faced his sister, and stepped backward, putting space between himself and her.

Karl pulled his Walther P38 from his side holster, raised his gun, and fired.

CHAPTER TWENTY

A Jewish man, one nearest to Karl, dropped to his knees, slumping over to the cold, brown ground. His warm, dark-red blood poured out from the single gunshot wound to his head. The dead man's wife and two young children erupted into screams as they fell to the ground, shaking their husband and father.

Karl realized that the youngest of the dead man's two children, a girl about five years of age, was the same little dark-haired girl who, only days before when he had trekked over to family camp for the first time to talk to Else, had asked him if she and her family were safe now. Though he was drunk when he met her, he still remembered her face, her innocence. And now, now that he had killed her father, what would his answer be to her question?

"Please," said the Standartenfuhrer, "tell me that you have a very good reason for disobeying a direct order. I told you to kill this Jew, and you killed a different one."

"Sir," began Karl, "I am very much hoping, at this moment, that you will believe it is a very good reason."

Two guards rushed over to the screaming family of the fallen man, guns drawn.

"No," the Standartenfuhrer said. "Let them be. Their cries fill me with great joy." He turned back to Karl. "Please, Engel, enlighten me."

"Well, sir, I believe in prolonging the suffering of the Jews. Since this girl, the one that you chose, is so young, she has more time to be whittled down to even less than she already is. Why break just her body, when we can also break her soul—I mean, if she had one. And, since you did order a death, I still gave you one. I do hope that you are not disappointed…sir."

The Standartenfuhrer thought for a moment, looking back and forth between the fallen man, the young girl that had been originally marked for death, and Karl, finally saying, "Disappointed? Absolutely, not. I like the way you think. I do wonder, however, how it is that they are the only family in this side of the camp with shaven heads." He pointed to Sarah, Miriam, and Else. "That is why I chose her. Obviously, they were not here to begin with. Who ordered their transfer?"

Sarah still squirmed in the guards' arms.

"I did, sir," said Karl. "So that they would write further of our benevolence in their letters."

The Standartenfuhrer smiled, clapping his hands, smiling like a little kid getting a new toy. "I love it! The rumors about you are not unfounded, Engel. You have a lot of initiative, and I am quite impressed with your ambition to further your career by making such a decision on your own, and even more impressed with your ingenuity. I also very much enjoy watching how quickly you think on your feet. Your calculations were quite fast." He waved his hand, ordering Sarah's release.

Karl glanced back over his shoulder as his younger sister ran to her mother's arms. Then he looked at the two young children begging for their daddy, the little girl and her slightly older sister, draped over their father's body.

"Thank you, sir," said Karl, now desperate to get his tour group out of family camp. "I'm very pleased to hear it. Now, if you'd like to follow me back this way, I can return you to--."

"Just a moment, Engel," said the Standartenfuhrer. "I think, however, that you underestimate even yourself."

"I'm afraid I don't understand, sir."

"Well," said the Nazi colonel, placing his arm around Karl's shoulders, walking toward the wailing family, "I asked you to kill one Jew, which you did, but you've actually killed three more than I wanted in the process. Like I said, you calculate very fast."

"How did I do that? I mean, kill three more, sir?"

"Since this is family camp, and you have permanently broken that family, they no longer belong here." The man snapped his fingers, and the two guards standing beside the dead man's family grabbed the children, followed by two more guards pulling the mother. The colonel cupped his hand to his ear as a train sounded in the distance. "They will now go to have their shower with the incoming Jews."

Karl walked in a daze beside the Standartenfuhrer, unable to completely fathom what had just taken place and his role in it. He listened to the young children cry for their daddy, focused especially on the youngest girl, the one who asked if she was safe. She also looked at him, her arms outstretched.

"Engel," said the Standartenfuhrer, "you are a natural-born Nazi. I think I'd like to speak to you in private, for a moment. Please, step over here."

The colonel pulled Karl aside, away from the visiting Nazis.

"I've heard a rumor that there may be an opening soon in the Camp Administrative Offices, in Berlin. I've also heard your father's name mentioned from time to time. Now, I've never met him, but I do know that he's very well-respected in certain circles, and we are all looking quite forward to his next, shall we say, project. It would be quite something to see father and son working together to bring peace to Germany, indeed all of Europe, seeing as how both of you have fallen into the same career field, so to speak."

"Yes, sir." Karl looked over the Nazi's shoulder, to the little girl being carried away.

"Very good, then. I look forward to seeing you again very soon."

"Yes, sir." Those two words were all the young Nazi's brain could muster.

"Comrades," said the Colonel, returning to the larger group, "I think this concludes our tour."

Following the Standartenfuhrer's lead, the other visitors turned around, and headed out of family camp.

"We can find our own way back, Engel" said the Standartenfuhrer. "Why don't you take the rest of the day off? You've earned it. Oh, and one more thing—make sure that these Jews are worked more than they are. I know that they were all cleaned up for my visit, but I care about clean soldiers, not clean Jews."

"Yes…sir."

Karl stood, dumbfounded, watching the visiting dignitaries laugh as they followed behind the screaming family, the dead father bein dragged, face down, between the two groups.

Karl put his hand to his pistol, unbuttoning the holster. He followed slowly behind the exiting group, taking a couple steps, in a zombie-like state.

"Karl," said Miriam, running up to him, her hands on his face. "Karl, snap out of it. I know what you're thinking. Don't do it. Don't do this."

He barely registered her presence.

"Son, you will only get yourself, and everyone else here killed. It will serve no purpose to strike him, any of them, down."

Karl finally drew his attention away from his moving target, looking into her watery eyes. His hand still rested on his gun.

"That's it," she said, her eyes locked onto his, her hands pulling his face down to hers. "Come back. Walk away from this."

A single tear broke away from his right eye.

"Come see me, later tonight," she said. "I need you to be strong, right now. Please, my boy, come back tonight."

Karl looked at her, like he was looking through her, and wandered off, the cries of the children and their mother, growing fainter in the distance as they headed to the shower.

CHAPTER TWENTY ONE

Karl returned that night, stumbling into Miriam's barracks, fueled, again, by Cognac. He was out of uniform, wearing black slacks, a white button shirt, and black tie. His gun was holstered at his side, and he carried a silver flask in his hand.

"What's everyone looking at?" he grumbled, noting all the pairs of eyes on him as he made his way down the middle aisle, toward his mother's bunk. "Don't you know I'll have you all killed? And I'll use only one bullet to do it."

Switching the flask from his right hand to his left, he reached down and unsnapped his holster. The nearby women moved back.

Miriam walked swiftly down the aisle, an intense determination on her face. With Karl's hand on his still-holstered Walther P38, she placed her hand over his.

"Let's talk in private," she said, her eyes locked on his like a sniper.

Turning around, she led him down the aisle, toward the back of the barracks, stopping suddenly when Sarah came out from between two bunks; the teen threw her arms around Karl. She stood there, crying, on his shoulder.

Karl slowly removed his hand from his gun, as his mother removed hers, and embraced his young sister. Karl's eyes welled. Then, as quickly as she had appeared, Sarah let go, and walked back to her bed.

Miriam grabbed the front of Karl's shirt and continued on, until they reached the shower room, the same where Albert and Else had their 'date.'

Then he saw her, Else, with her big, brown eyes so visible in the moonlight with her still-short, but softer-looking regrowth of brown hair. It pained him to look at her.

"What do you want with me, Miriam?" he asked.

"First, I want to say thank you. I know you don't want to hear it, and I understand why. It's not easy to be thankful when an entire family…" She stopped herself, and refocused. "Second, I wanted to make sure you were okay. I can clearly see that you're not."

"Okay? Okay? Fuck no, I'm not okay!" Karl paced around the room, placing his hand on the walls at times to steady himself, taking sips from his flask.

"You saved Sarah," said Miriam. "You saved your sister. I'm sorry for what you had to do, but you didn't know what would come of it. Believe me, my heart breaks for having lost so many of our people. Those are generations more that cannot be replaced." Miriam suddenly stopped talking, and began sobbing.

"An entire family—gone," he said. "For the sake of one. I'm not sorry that Sarah is alive, but…" He closed his eyes tight, leaning against a dark wall. "Don't you hear it? Don't you hear the children screaming? They scream here, outside, in family camp. They scream in the trains. They scream…in the showers."

Karl placed his hand back on his holster. "Ask Albert about it. He hears it all the time." He took his hand off, and took another drink from the flask. "How much more do I have to hear?"

"Karl," said Else.

"And, you," he said, not giving her a chance to say what was coming. "No matter what I do, I can never rid myself of that first night. Not that it matters, because, as you saw earlier, no matter what I do, you're all going to die." His hand dropped to his side, swinging next to the gun. "And so will I."

"I forgive you," Else said.

Karl's tear-filled eyes blinked, letting the saltwater fall. "What?"

"I forgive you. And, I'm sorry that I told Albert about it. I was wrong."

Miriam walked out, as Else walked over. Karl trembled.

"Your father," she began, "your real father, owned a bakery in the neighborhood."

"What are you talking about?"

"I'm telling you how I know your family. I'm telling you a little bit about me. He was very kind to everyone who entered his shop, often taking less for his bread and other items than what he was selling them for, or what he should have. And, Albert worked there. He needed to help out as much as possible because, you know, your dad's condition—with his hand. Anyway, that's how he and I know each other; it's how your mom and sister know me.

"My family has…," Else continued, pausing. "My family *had* little money, so I would often trade my pictures for some bread."

The Camp

"You take pictures?"

"I *draw* pictures. I use different materials, any kind of medium."

"You're an artist."

"Photographers are artists, too, but, yes. Anyway, Jakob would take my drawings, or paintings, and hang them in his bakery, giving me bread for my family in return."

"Did you go to art school? How good are you?"

"No, I did not attend art school. I always wanted to go, but my family was unable to send me. I don't know if I'm good, or not, but your father was kind to take my drawings, anyway. But, this was all before everyone was moved to the ghetto. When that happened, Albert and I saw each other a little, on the streets, from time to time, but that was all. My parents died there. I then saw your family less and less, until we came here, to the camp. Your mother has been taking care of me, Sarah, and herself ever since.

"She worries constantly about her family—her daughter, her son...both her sons. Please, Karl, whatever you may be thinking, as a result of what happened today, don't. She's lost her husband, your father, and Albert is on the other side of the camp. You are the only link she has to him, and you are the son that she thought was lost for good. Now, you're back.

"What happened today was both a miracle and a tragedy. We will help you get through it. You mentioned before that you don't know what it means to be Jewish, and I responded unfairly to that statement. You need to understand that being Jewish is about so many things, one of those being community. Yes, Sarah was saved, but four others were lost in her place. Everyone here is mourning that. You feel like you're alone; you're not. I know that you were making a choice when you helped Sarah, I know that you were trying to choose life. I can see, now, that you wouldn't have killed that man if the Germans hadn't put you in that position."

"Yeah, well, if community is so important to Jews, then why do some enjoy being Kapos? I mean they actually seem to like what they do. I've seen the look in their eyes when they're hitting and kicking their own people. They like abusing their own, sometimes more harshly than Nazis do. I've seen Jews kill other Jews to save themselves. That's not community, that's self-preservation. How do you explain that?"

"I don't know."

"Maybe," said Miriam, reentering the shower room, "it's because of what the Nazis have designed here. This camp is not like the rest of society, out there in the real world. In this little world that the Nazis have created, not everything, or everyone, is black and white. The Nazis have purposefully caused a breakdown in the Jewish community. By taking away our rights, not just religious, but human rights, some parts of our community have begun to collapse, parts meaning individuals. In times like these, in situations like this, Jewish or not, any community will suffer the same fate. We are turning against ourselves, and that's exactly what the Nazis want.

"That does not mean, though, that everyone will react like so many Kapos have. I have seen a couple of very kind Kapos in this camp. Not everyone will respond the same. People are still people, human beings are still human beings, and all are individuals with their own driving needs, wants, and desires. I, too, have seen an 'every man for himself' mentality, just as you have, but I've also witnessed one Nazi begin to fight against what he's been taught, and strive to become a better man. Not all Jews are like the Kapos you talk about, just like, I now believe, not all Nazis are beyond redemption."

Karl exhaled for what seemed to him like the first time in weeks.

"I don't really know you," said Else, stepping closer, "but I want to believe that the night in the shower wasn't really you. I want to believe it was because you were drunk, and your friends were involved. I want to believe that there is something different about you. That you would still realize the things you were doing were wrong, even if you never found out who you really are. I don't know. I'm still scared to believe any of that.

"And, I'm sure you're right, that we'll all die here, but you gave us some hope in humanity. Yes, a family was killed today, but—sometimes, I think the ones who die immediately, are the lucky ones."

"Else--," began Karl.

"We have to go now. I'll talk to you later." She walked toward the shower room exit, grabbed Miriam's hand, then stopped, and turned. "You look nice, tonight."

Karl watched Else and Miriam leave as he slid down the wall behind him, sat on the cold floor, and cried.

CHAPTER TWENTY TWO

Karl, having spent the previous night sleeping in the shower, awoke, hungover, and resigned to the idea that his family, even Else, would die soon. He felt it was time to make his peace with his brother. By the time he had changed into his uniform, and reached the crematoria, however, his brother was already gone.

"What do you mean he's not here?" Karl asked one of the guards, his mind racing. "Is he in the shower?"

He raced to the latched door, preparing to open it, a desperate fear coming over him that his brother was leaving this world without having heard Karl apologize for everything.

"Stop!" yelled the guard. "You'll let the gas out! He's not in there. He hasn't been terminated. Three other guards came to get him. Jeez, are you trying to kill us all?"

"Three guards?" Karl asked the question, knowing full well what the answer was.

"Yeah, they said they were friends of yours. I didn't care. They did tell me tell you, in case in you came looking, they'd be at our barracks."

"Thanks."

Reaching the SS dorm where he, Klaus, Wilhelm, and Hans had been assigned, all he had to do was follow the laughter to its origin to find Albert. Karl walked down the warm hallway to his own room and opened the door.

"What the hell is this?" he asked, finding Albert in his underwear dancing to the music of Frederic Chopin, his arms wide open, grasping his phantom partner. The humiliation and, at the same time, acceptance, on his face said it all.

"What?" asked Klaus, sitting on Karl's bed. "We're just having a little fun. We haven't hurt your pet Jew. Please, come in, and don't forget to close the door. We wouldn't want the wrong people to know he's in here."

"Yeah," said Wilhelm. "We didn't think we had to ask to borrow your stuff, since we're all friends."

Karl saw the two bottles of Jaeger on his dresser, one empty, the other nearly there. He shut the door behind him.

"Okay," he said, picking the record player's needle up from the vinyl album, "that's enough. More Jews will be here early in the morning, and he's got to be well-rested to do his work. I need to get some sleep, too."

"We don't like that idea," said Klaus, standing. "In fact, we don't like the way you've been acting lately. You used to be fun, a bit too serious, but you wouldn't have acted like this. But we think all the praise you've received lately has gone to your head." He paused. "Or, is there more to this Jew than what you're saying? And, put the music back on. We have a guest coming, and need this party to continue."

"Someone else is coming here?" Karl asked. "Who?"

Klaus just smiled. He got up, put the needle back on the record, and sat back on the bed.

Karl thought fast. "I'm very sorry, my friends. My father has been on my back about making him look better. Of course, there's nothing to this Jew, because he means nothing. Like you said, he's a pet, that's it."

"Oh, I've got a great idea," Hans said. "Let's dress him up."

"What are you talking about?" asked Klaus.

"Well, he kinda looks like Karl, anyway, let's see what he looks like in his uniform."

"A Jew in an SS uniform?" asked Wilhelm. "No more Jaeger for you!"

The three guards laughed as Klaus reached in Karl's closet and pulled out a gray uniform. "Let's do it," he said.

"I don't think that's such a good--," said Karl, stopping when he saw Klaus stare at him coldly. "Fine. Go ahead. Tarnish our good name. I don't care."

A sudden knock at the door increased the tension in Karl's body.

"You'll want to answer that," said Klaus.

Karl shot him a nervous look.

"Don't worry. Do you really think we'd tell someone we didn't trust to come up here, and get ourselves in trouble? Just answer the door."

The Camp

Hans and Wilhelm picked through Karl's closet for a pair of shiny boots, as the latter opened the door.

Standing in the hallway, still wearing her SS garb, was a young, blue-eyed woman, about medium height, with her blonde hair pulled back in a ponytail. She smiled, and Karl realized he'd seen her before.

"This is Claudia," said Klaus, still sitting on Karl's bed. "She works on the women's side of the camp, obviously. I figured you needed a distraction from your…distractions."

"You were right, Klaus," Claudia said, entering the room, and shutting the door, "he is very handsome." She ran her hand across Karl's face.

Karl's thoughts stumbled in his head, unsure of what to do next.

"Is that the Jew you mentioned?" she asked, walking over to a now nude Albert. She pointed at his genitals, and laughed. "His thing looks ugly, being circumcised. I would never touch a Jew's thing. So dirty. How do they stand doing it with each other?"

"I know," said Klaus. "Disgusting, isn't it?"

Karl's eyes met Albert's as the former looked away, ashamed of what he was hearing, full of pity for what Albert was going through.

"Claudia," Klaus began, "has a lot in common with you, Karl. She killed her first Jew woman recently, and has quite the reputation on the women's side, herself. That's why I picked her for you."

"I'm sorry, Claudia," said Karl, "but I'm not looking for anyone, at this time."

Hans and Wilhelm, having gotten a full uniform together, began dressing Albert.

"But, we'd make such a good pair," Claudia said, smiling, exuding sex appeal as she slinked toward Karl. "We could rise through the ranks together, making pure German babies along the way."

"Make babies? You just met me. I'm sorry, but I'm just not your type."

Moments later, Albert stood in the middle of the room, Karl's Nazi uniform hanging loose from his body. No one laughed.

"It's even more incredible than I thought," said Klaus. "The resemblance is amazing."

"Yeah," Hans said, "he looks just like Karl. I mean, like looking at his twin. If this Jew were actually a person, a real German, I'd say he *is* Karl's twin."

"Except, he's smaller," said Wilhelm. "Not much meat left on him. We should call him Little Karl."

"Yes, Little Karl!" said Klaus. "That's perfect!"

"I don't care how much he looks like Karl," Claudia said, "I still wouldn't touch a Jew."

"Okay," began Karl, "you've had your fun, and you're ruining the uniform. Let's take it off, now." He moved to unbutton Albert's shirt. "I'm so tired of the comparison."

"Wait," Klaus said. "I've got a better idea."

"What now?" Karl felt exasperated.

"Follow me."

Klaus grabbed Albert by the arm, and began leading him out of the room.

"Whoa!" Karl said, jumping in front of the door. "You can't take him outside dressed like that. Somebody will see."

"It'll be fine. It's early. Besides, who's going to question five guards?"

"If someone finds out we've got a Jew in our uniform, we'll all be court-martialed."

"It'll only be for a few minutes."

Karl saw the impatience grow in Klaus' eyes, and knew that if he didn't go along with his friend's plan, he and Albert would both be in danger.

"Fine," said Karl, moving from the doorway. "But, where are you taking him?"

"I just want to see if Little Karl is anything like Big Karl."

CHAPTER TWENTY THREE

Albert clopped down the stairs of the SS dorm, and out the door, behind Klaus, and followed by Karl, Wilhelm, Hans, and Claudia. Panic ran rampant in Karl's body. The mid-March morning sun seemed brighter than moments before, highlighting their presence for all to see.

The group rounded a corner of the building where Wilhelm handed a cigarette out to each person, including Albert.

"I don't smoke," Albert said. Everyone but he and Karl laughed.

"You see that chimney over there?" Klaus asked, pointing toward one of the crematoria. "You'll smoke soon enough."

Klaus' chilling words ran through Karl.

"Karl's right," Klaus continued. "We can't just drag him around in public. Hans, fetch me a Jew."

Watching Hans scamper off, everyone remained quiet, smoking their cigarettes, except for Albert. Karl wondered what could possibly be going through his brother's mind. He also wondered what Klaus was up to. Karl looked to his side, and saw Claudia still eyeballing him, smiling. He shook his head and looked away.

"That's okay," she said. "I like it when men play hard to get. You know why? Because, when it comes down to it, you're really not that hard to get. When you do give in, though, you think it was your decision. Men act more manly when they think they're in charge, so go ahead, act any way you want." Her pretty, white smile, framed by cherry-red lips, never faded.

Hans returned a few minutes later behind a young Jewish woman. Klaus removed his gun from his holster, handing it to Albert.

"Now," said Klaus, "kill the Jew bitch."

"Please, no," said the woman, falling to her knees, crying, grabbing Albert's gray-uniformed legs. "I beg you. Please."

Albert tried to give the gun back.

"Uh-uh, Little Karl," Klaus said, "you kill her, then you can give it back, and return to your barracks."

"I know this woman," said Claudia.

Albert looked at the pistol in his hand, took a step back, and pointed it at Klaus. The Nazi, along with Hans, Wilhelm, and Claudia, burst out in laughter.

"Please, no," said Wilhelm, mocking the Jewish woman. "I beg you. Please."

"Yes, Jew," Hans said, "please don't kill us."

"I do know you don't I, Jew woman?" Claudia continued, easing her laughter.

Albert, his hand shaking, turned the gun on Karl. The three male guards laughed harder.

"Little Karl is going to shoot Big Karl," said Klaus, barely getting his words out. "You see? This is why I signed up for this. Where else would you get entertainment like this?"

Karl stood there, unmoving, his eyes on Albert's, ready to die.

"I know who you are," said Claudia. "Of course, I don't know your name, because I don't care to know your name, but I've heard a rumor about you. You're pregnant, aren't you?"

The woman on her knees didn't respond. Albert suddenly lowered the gun.

"Oh, no, you don't," Klaus continued. "You may look like him, but you don't have a bit of Karl's heart. Still, you're not getting out of this. I still want to see what it looks like. Kill that Jew. I don't care if she is pregnant."

"How was she able to get pregnant here?" asked Hans.

"She didn't get pregnant here, you idiot," Claudia said. "She arrived only a week ago, and she's not that far along."

"I can't," Albert said.

"Sure, you can. And, here's how I know that you can." Klaus stepped closer. "I saw you, before Karl moved you to be a Sonderkommando, talking to some women through the fence. I suspect, that if I were to look into it further, that they may be close to you. Family, perhaps? So, if you want me to continue to look the other way, which I do only because of Karl, then you will raise that gun, and shoot her." Klaus walked to the woman, and placed his finger on her forehead. "Right here."

Albert's tears streamed down as he looked to his brother. Karl stood, motionless, unable to intercede, knowing Albert was looking to him for help. Karl could only think about what he had to do to save Sarah the day before. His pity for Albert was overwhelming. Karl looked away.

The woman, still on her knees, having calmed herself enough to listen to the conversation, burst into pleas again, when Claudia suddenly stepped forward.

"Here, Little Karl, let me help you." The female Nazi pulled her pistol, and shot the Jewish woman in the lower abdomen. "Now, you can let her suffer, or you can kill her. She's going to die anyway, but you determine how quickly and how long she'll be in pain."

The young Jewish woman remained on her knees, doubled over, screaming, her hands covering her wound.

Karl took a couple of steps back, astounded by what was happening.

"Forgive me," said Albert.

A shot rang out, and the woman fell backward, hitting the wall behind her. Blood ran down her forehead, past her eyes, nose, mouth, and dripped from her chin.

"Very good, Little Karl," said Klaus, clapping. "But, you're still no Big Karl." He took his smoking weapon from Albert, and holstered it. "If you do have family here, they get to suffer another day. Hans and Wilhelm, get the dead Jew out of here. Karl, you can have your pet back, now."

"I'll see you later, Karl," said Claudia. The pretty blonde kept smiling.

Karl pulled Albert, catatonic and zombie-like, from the spot around the corner, back into the SS building, and into his room.

Sitting Albert on his bed, and bending down to help him get out of the red-splattered, gray Nazi uniform, Karl stopped, for a moment. He stood, stepping back, to get another, longer look at Albert in the uniform.

Karl began thinking, though he didn't quite know what he thinking about. He just felt that there was something he was looking at, something he was seeing, in that moment, that he hadn't seen before. Something he hadn't noticed outside.

He bent back down, and helped his brother, his entranced twin, get undressed, and slip back into the black-and-white striped pajamas.

CHAPTER TWENTY FOUR

Karl stood watch in family camp later that day, having returned Albert to his own barracks. Lost in thought, he continued to wonder what it was about Albert, sitting on his bed in the SS dorm, that wouldn't leave him alone.

What was it? he thought, vigorously working his mind to retrieve the picture of Albert in the Nazi uniform. *What was I looking at? What the hell did I see in the room that I didn't see outside?*

His rifle slung over his shoulder, Karl watched a group of ten kids, their clothes all muddied, playing football. It was nearly spring, and the children in family camp were taking advantage of the warmer weather as best they could. Still, though he was watching them, his head moving around as they did, he wasn't exactly paying attention. Mostly, his eyes drifted toward the ground as he recalled the look of Albert sitting on the guard's bed—all the previous events of the morning that led up to that moment, Karl tried to gloss over, and forget.

They were right, the guys were right, when they said that he looked even more like me in the uniform than he does in those damn pajamas.

The kids moved down the grassless field, toward him. As they progressed, the group passed in front of Else, who stood far afield, her hand raised just above her waist, waving at him.

Karl, moving deeper within his own thoughts, stopped following the kids' movements. His ears tuned out all noise, and his eyes continued to see only Else in her white dress. He blinked repeatedly, refocusing his gaze, as if the girl across the field were some kind of specter, haunting him, like the memory of Albert, as he realized that somehow, for some reason, there was a connection between her and how his brother looked that morning. Suddenly, the world stopped, and everything that occurred outside his mind, washed away.

It's not possible. It can't be that simple.

Karl suddenly snapped out of his inner canyon when the kids on the field gathered around him, yelling. He turned to look behind him and saw a boy, one of the players, on the other side of the fence, running to retrieve the football. It had landed about halfway between the fence and the surrounding forest. Karl then realized that the spacing between the fencing was meant to keep adults contained, but had never been designed to keep children in, as family camp was never part of the original design. Something that, clearly, the inept guards in family camp still hadn't noticed.

Karl spun back around to see if any other nearby guards had noticed the commotion. It seemed, at the moment, that no one else was watching the scene unfold, except for the boys, and Else.

"Hey, all you kids, quiet," Karl said. They all immediately hushed as the guard had commanded.

The boy reached the ball, picked it up, and started back toward the fence, when Karl shook his head. The boy stopped. Karl reached to his side, and drew his sidearm. The children that were gathered around him gasped.

"Everyone scatter…and look busy," he whispered to the group.

His eyes oscillated, only his eyes, checking his peripheral vision, then he cautiously advanced his head in each direction, making sure he still wasn't being watched.

Suddenly, he let his gun fall to the ground. "Oh, no," he said, calmly, even somewhat sarcastically, just in case there did happen to be someone behind him within earshot. "I dropped my gun. I have to pick it up."

Karl gave the boy a wink and nod, then turned his back, bent over, and picked up the Walther P38. When he stood, and turned back around, the boy was gone. Only the ball remained.

"Hey!" yelled a guard, running over. "What the hell are you doing? You just let a kid escape out there."

"Did I?" Karl asked, looking around. "I don't see any kid."

"That's because he escaped, you idiot! He's gone!"

"Well, if you saw him, and I didn't, doesn't that mean that *you* let him escape?"

"Hey, smartass, I heard you were supposed to be this great guard, that we could all learn something from you. Three guards are out sick today, and they

The Camp

sent you, just you, to replace all of them. And you can't even watch a bunch of kids."

"Well, I still see a bunch of kids here. Like I said, you're the only one that saw one of them run off into the forest. So what are you going to do about that?"

"We're going to have to go get him."

"Oh, I'm not sure how you're going to justify sending a bunch of guards, into a large forest, after one kid."

The guard huffed. "You may be great where you come from, but you're too soft for this side of the camp. You are no Nazi; you're a woman, a kindergarten teacher. Except, you lose kids, so you're a terrible kindergarten teacher."

"Hmm. So sorry you feel that way. I will try to work harder to make sure that these kids do not take down the entire Nazi regime. I'll also try to keep a better eye on those invisible children that you see heading into the woods."

"You do that. And leave that damn ball out there. They shouldn't be allowed to play games here, anyway."

"Now, you can't really do that, either. We're trying to keep these Jews happy so that they write happy letters. If you leave the ball out there, you're only working against the very idea of family camp." Karl stepped closer to the man. "Are you intentionally setting out to damage what our leaders are trying to accomplish?"

The other Nazi grew more irritated, pacing in a circle before he finally decided to let a girl retrieve the football, watching the child himself until she came back to the fence.

"You will not guard this side of the camp again," the guard said, marching off.

Karl felt the calm within swirl away as a storm swelled up inside, pushing aside any goodwill he had left for the other guard. Karl followed the man, nearing the rear of the last of the barracks in family camp. He stretched his fingers as they swung back and forth at his side, quietly storing the build-up of potential energy.

Waiting until they were behind the building, out of sight, Karl grabbed the back of the man's neck and thrust his head into the wooden frame of the housing. The other guard, knocked senseless, fell to the ground, and rolled onto his back, opening his eyes, finding his mouth covered by Karl's hand, and staring down the barrel of a gun.

"Now, let's get something straight," said Karl. "I don't like to be threatened, and, I'm pretty sure, you don't want to die."

The guard quickly shook his head, as Karl slowly mimicked.

"Good. So here's the deal—you're going to keep your mouth shut, and I'm going to keep this bullet in the gun. Also, if you *ever* speak to me again, even so much as to tell me 'guten Morgen,' your family won't be able to identify your body, because there will be no body to identify. Do you understand?"

The man, blood seeping down his face from his forehead, nodded.

"Excellent. Now, get up, and make sure you tell people that you tripped and hit a rock. And walk calmly out of here; don't run."

The guard nodded again, jumped to his feet, and walked away as quickly as he could.

Karl, his inner calm returning, smiled.

CHAPTER TWENTY FIVE

That evening, Karl waltzed into the women's barracks, and asked Else to speak with him in private. She agreed, though her departure was delayed by Miriam, who pulled Karl aside, into a nearby corner. She stood on her toes, leaning into him.

"At least you don't smell like alcohol." Miriam flattened her feet. "Son, should you be doing this?"

"No, I'm not drunk, thanks for noticing" he said, smiling. "And, what do you mean, should I be doing this? Doing what?"

"Let's ignore that I could just be talking about how you simply *feel* about Else, for a moment. What I'm really talking about is you actually coming over here and spending so much time with her, singling her out. Some of the women are starting to talk. You don't think that you might be drawing too much attention to yourself? Or her? Maybe putting her in danger, knowing there are some people who could, and possibly would, use that information to help themselves?"

"I don't know what you mean. I don't feel anything." He looked around the barracks. "And, she's not in danger, because she's being pulled out by me—who's going to rat on a guard? But, just out of curiosity, what are they saying?"

"They're wondering why a Nazi guard is so interested in a Jewish girl. Some here know about Albert, and they've remarked about the resemblance between you two. Now, no one here knows your secret, as far as I know, but they are talking. And don't act like you don't care about her, in a certain way. I may have seen you for the first time in eighteen years only a month ago, but I gave birth to you. A mother knows her son."

"I can take care of myself, and I've been taking care of all of you without any trouble, haven't I? Everything's fine."

"I'm just saying that this isn't the normal place and time for a budding romance. I know you care about her, but you're putting your life at risk more than it already is. You need to watch what you're doing."

"Look, I don't know if you've heard, but I'm pretty much untouchable now. One of the guards over here tried to get me in trouble because I let a kid escape. His complaint went…nowhere. And, why can't I feel something for Else? Even if I weren't coming over here, you said that I shouldn't even feel anything for her. You think Albert is the only one good enough for her? Why? Because he doesn't wear this uniform? Because he wasn't raised by Jew-hating parents when he was given away as a baby?"

"No, son, that's not what I mean. I just mean that, even though you now know the truth about you, you're still not like her. You and Else are worlds apart; she and Albert have so much in common, they already have something of a past. Besides, the rest of us are already dead—you're not."

"So it *is* because of the path my life took, before I learned the truth. He got to know her before I did, so he has the right to her. Finders, keepers, is that what you're saying? Besides, she and I may be worlds apart, but at least I can see her whenever I want. Albert can't get near her without my help, so what good does it do him, or her, for me to step out of the picture?"

Miriam looked away.

"I don't want to talk about this anymore, anyway" he said, starting to walk away. "She forgave me for that night in the shower. You're ruining my good mood."

Miriam grabbed his arm, pulling him back.

"Son, forget everything else that was just said—do you understand that the only way for your secret to truly be safe, is to completely, and permanently, sever any connection to us? You have to remove any trace of us. The rest of us are going to die; if they discover who you really are, so will you. Do you understand that? I know you told her that you'd protect her, but you can't protect her from everything, not in a place like this. You're still a low-ranking Nazi; even you have your limitations."

Karl stared at her, pried her hand from his arm, and walked away, leaving his mother alone in the corner. He moved up behind Else, whispered for her to follow, and they left the building, returning to the shower area.

"Your mother is very worried," she said, as they entered the building. "She will not say about what, but I can tell."

"Yeah, I just talked to her. It's nothing. I have it under control. I've got my superiors eating out of the palm of my hand. And I'm allowed to feel whatever I want."

"What are you talking about?"

"Nothing. I'm not worried about it, so you shouldn't be, either. Forget I said anything."

"Karl," she began, stepping closer to him in the dark, placing her hand on his arm. He shivered, goosebumps rising all over his body, underneath his uniform. "What's going to happen to us? To me? Your family?"

"I don't know," he said, unable to think of anything else in that second beyond her touch.

"We're all going to die, aren't we? Just like you said."

Karl's emotions stirred in him like a storm created by the headlong collision of two different fronts: the happiness he felt in the moment of her touch, and the despair of the truth of her situation.

"What is it with you and my mother? I came here in a really good mood."

"Karl, we don't know what a good mood is, not anymore. It's been so long since I've felt good about anything. Please, try to understand it from our perspective."

Karl kept quiet, trying to bring back the feeling he had a moment before, when she laid her hand on him.

"How is Albert?" she asked.

The feeling was gone.

"Fine," he said. "He had a rough morning, though."

"What do you mean? Is he okay?"

"Nothing. He's fine. I'm working on it. You have feelings for him, don't you?"

"Yes, I do." She paused for a few seconds. "And--."

"I have it all under control. I think. I don't know. Maybe she's right."

"What does any of that mean? I still don't understand what you're talking about?"

"I don't know."

"Are you okay?" She touched him again.

"I don't know." Karl walked toward the door, standing for a moment with his hands in his pockets. He heard her feet shuffle across the floor in his direction. "It's time for me to get back to my dorm," he continued. "Before I go, though, I want to give you something."

He turned, walking slowly back toward her, pulling his hands from his pockets, and placing them in hers.

"What is this?" she asked, opening her hands, squinting to spy in the dark what he'd placed in them. In her palms were a piece of paper, and a lump of coal.

"You said you were an artist. We don't have any real paint or anything else like that here, so I had to ask around to find out what other materials artists work with. These are all I could find."

"The guards have paper and coal just lying around?"

"Don't worry about where I got the coal," he said, staring at the black lump in her hand. "I whittled it down for you. Hopefully you can create something good out of it."

"I'll see what I can do."

Else placed both items in one hand, and reached out to touch him again. Karl backed away, moving again toward the door.

"I'll take you back, now," he said, in a somber tone.

Karl escorted Else to her barracks door, then walked to his dorm, his head held low, unable to retrieve the memory, or feeling, of her touch.

CHAPTER TWENTY SIX

Karl stood at the train depot, on the first day of spring, ushering newly arriving Jews into the separate lines to be inspected, when his mind began to wander.

She touched me…twice, he thought. He eyes remained open, his conscious mind and body working on autopilot, going through the motions of moving the surviving Jews, all the lost souls, from the cattle cars to the platform, so the doctors could do their work.

God, her hand, on my arm, touching my sleeve…her skin so close to mine. She wanted to touch me.

Karl's heart pounded, picturing her face, her hand on his arm. He stood at the head of the line, and closed his eyes, letting the short, bespectacled doctor take over. Karl's brain began creating new, false images, of her hand going places that it hadn't the previous night: the warmth of her palm meeting his cheek, her fingertips sliding over his ear as her hand glided to the back of his neck, and she leaned in, her lips nearly reaching his…

"Karl?"

So lost in thought, he hadn't noticed that Wilhelm and Hans had come up to him, and were standing there, trying to get his attention.

"What?" he asked, annoyed.

"Hey," Hans said, "you seen Klaus?"

"No. I'm a little busy here." Karl didn't bother turning to face them.

"We know, and we're sorry to bother you, but it's important. We wanted you to know that we had no part in it. We thought it was a crazy idea to begin with."

"What are you talking about?" Karl rolled his eyes, and turned around. Everything, all the drama, was getting old. He had grown tired of all of it, yet he now gave them his full attention.

"Klaus called Berlin about you," said Wilhelm. "He was convinced--."

"He what?" Karl yelled, cutting off the guard. "What the fuck do you mean he called Berlin about me?"

"Shhh, keep your voice down," Hans said. "Everyone's looking over here."

"Let them look. You two had better start talking. What's he convinced of? Who did he call?"

"He was sure there was some kind of connection between you and that Jew," continued Wilhelm. "That you two were somehow related. He called a friend of his in the city, someone who works for the government."

"And? Who the hell did he talk to?"

"Someone who could dig up your birth certificate there, but don't worry, everything's fine. The certificate says what we all already knew—that your parents are really your parents. I guess he figured that even your father couldn't fake that."

"That's a dumb statement, of course my parents are really my parents. I was never worried about it. Just because the guy looks like me doesn't mean we're related." *Klaus obviously doesn't know my father*, he thought. *He creates perfect families.*

"He's okay, now," Hans said, "but, we wanted to tell you first, before you found out from him, so that you wouldn't think we had anything to do with it."

"So now," said Wilhelm, "he's convinced that there is no connection. The Jew just happens to look like you, and he figures you're keeping him around for entertainment, like giving him the job as Sonderkommando."

"Yeah," said Hans, "giving him the worst job you can give a Jew—that's pretty funny."

"When I see him…" said Karl, his anger manifesting as he balled his fists.

"No," pleaded Hans, "please, don't do anything."

"Yeah," Wilhelm said, "you're not supposed to know he called. He wasn't going to tell you. He didn't find anything. Everything turned out okay. So, no need to bring it up."

"He'll know that we told you," Hans said.

"So you want me to keep quiet about him trying to dig up dirt on me?"

"Yes."

"No," said Karl.

Suddenly, Klaus walked upon the scene.

"Hey, guys, what's going--?"

"The next time you want to investigate whether I'm a dirty fucking Jew, you'd better place a call to Hitler for some personal protection."

"Karl," began Klaus, staring at Wilhelm and Hans, his face reddening, "people are starting to talk."

"Yeah? The only ones I hear talking are these two, telling me what you did. Who the hell else is talking? And, what are they saying?"

"Other guards. Prisoners. They're saying that you're protecting him, the Jew who looks like you. That you visit the same women, over in family camp, all the time. It is weird that he looks so much like you, especially when he's in our uniform."

"Look around," Karl said, "does it look like I can protect anyone here, even if I wanted to? So, you decided to believe them, over me. And, call Berlin. It was your idea to put him in the fucking uniform."

"I know, but--."

"But, nothing! Leave my Jews, and me, the hell alone!"

Karl stormed off, leaving his post, but hadn't made it far before Claudia caught up to him, her uniform pulled tight against her body.

"Where are you going?" she asked.

"Away. What do you want?"

"To ask you a question."

"You already did." He kept walking, trying to leave her behind.

"I just wanted to know if you've ever heard what happens to guards who are intimate with those...things."

He stopped in his tracks. "What are you getting at? What have *you* heard?"

"Nothing," she said, moving in close, her red lips nearing his, then backing away. "It's just that I really like you, and I'd hate for anyone to get the wrong idea about you. I mean, I know that you aren't involved with any of those insects, but someone else may think that you are, someone in command. I know that it's one of the few rules around here that absolutely cannot be broken. Careers are ruined for such things. Not to mention what could happen to the Jew that's caught. Hmm, much worse than the normal stuff—sent to a certain Block in the camp, I hear.

"But, don't worry, I want you to know that I care, and I'm looking out for you, making sure that no one spreads any false rumors. I think you and I really have something special going here."

"Thanks. Are you finished?"

"Yes." Claudia took a few steps back. "See you later?" she asked, smiling.

Karl turned, resuming his exit, though at a slower pace now. He looked back as he continued, over his shoulder, and saw her still standing there, smiling at him.

She's right, he thought. *Miriam's right. This is all so out of control. I just need to stay the hell away from everyone for a while. Especially…Else.*

CHAPTER TWENTY SEVEN

Hours turned into days as Karl agonized over what to do about his visitations when finally, on the cusp of April, unable to keep himself from going and a week after his confrontation with Klaus and Claudia, with everything seeming quiet, Karl entered the women's barracks, and exited with Else. He had her close her eyes, resting her hand on his bicep, as he led her through the night.

"Where are we going?" she asked, with a shy, slight smile.

"It's a surprise." His grin was bigger. "Well, where we're going isn't really a surprise, so much as what's there. We're going to the same place we usually go; the only place we really can go."

"It's been a while since I've seen you. I was beginning to wonder..."

"Wonder what?"

"If I was ever going to see you again."

"I wasn't sure about that, myself."

"What do you mean?" she asked, her voice raised a little.

"Nothing. It's not important."

"I've been thinking...there's something I want to tell you," said Else.

"There's something I want to tell you, too, but hold that thought, and open your eyes."

Else gasped as they entered the shower room and Karl led her to a large, tin washtub, already filled with water, that sat in the middle of the cold, concrete floor. A single light glowed from an oil burning lamp in a corner.

"Feel the water," he said.

She bent down, sticking the tips of her fingers in. "It's warm," she said, smiling bigger than he'd ever seen. She dipped the entire length of her fingers in, running them back and forth in the water, small ripples lapping the sides of the basin. "How did you manage to get warm water?"

"I have my ways."

"Is it to wash my dress? It's so dirty, now." She looked down, running her wet hand over the bottom half, trying to clean away the soil on the fabric.

"No," he said, laughing. He pulled a small vial, and a small bar of soap, out of his pocket. "It's to wash you, not your dress. This is shampoo," he said, holding up the vial. "There's also a towel on the floor, on the other side of the tub."

Else threw her hands up to cover her open mouth, obviously self-aware of her own shocked expression, as her eyes welled.

"Really? I get to take a warm bath?"

He nodded.

"What are you going to do? Where will you be?"

"I'll be right outside making sure no one comes in."

"Are you sure that you have to be…outside?" Her brown doe-like eyes dropped to the floor, then moved slowly back up to his.

"I…I think it's best. You can tell me whatever it was you wanted to say, after your bath."

Karl stepped out the building's door, leaving Else to undress, and sit in the warm tub. Though he made honest attempts to not picture her, unclothed, his mind just wouldn't follow orders.

Images of her slipping her worn, white dress off, one shoulder, then the other, flooded his brain. Bending down as she pushed it to the floor, stepping out, one foot at a time. Moving her underwear to her knees as she alternated their bending, they finally fell freely to the cold cement.

Else's nude body floated, in his mind, across the floor, to the tub where she set one soft, pale leg in, then the other, finally slipping, and sinking, into the warm water. He closed his eyes, able to hear the water from inside drip back into the tub, falling from, what he imagined to be her lathered calf.

He shivered.

"Karl," whispered Else, from inside.

"Yeah?" he called, poking his head in just enough to hear, and be heard. Several seconds passed before she responded.

"I…I need your help with something."

Are you sure? he thought about saying, but didn't.

Karl went back into the building, crossing the floor, past her clothes, to the tub where Else relaxed. He saw her, no longer in his mind, but in all her infinite, unimagined beauty. And he knew that he was seeing her like this because she wanted him to.

"What do you need?" he asked, softly.

"Would you mind washing my hair?"

He said not a word, knowing that she was quite capable of performing the task herself. He only rolled up his sleeves, and knelt behind her. Cupping his hands together, he poured water over her short, chestnut brown hair. Emptying the little bottle of shampoo into one hand, he exhaled into it, trying to warm the liquid.

Karl quickly, but gently, ran his hands, this way and that, over her soft, wet hair, now about an inch long, forming a lather with the shampoo. He worked his fingers through and through, back and forth, spreading the cleanser around, massaging her dry scalp, trying to get out any insects and dirt that may have accumulated. The camp was notorious for lice, which was only aided by the infrequent showering that was allowed, even in family camp.

What the hell am I doing? he thought, as he knelt there, washing the nude Jewish woman's hair. *If we were caught right now, I would be okay, I'd lose my career, but I'd be safe, physically. But, Else…God what they would do to her. Why am I putting her in danger like this? Why can't I stop myself? Why can't I seem to listen to people telling me to stop? Claudia's right, Else would be taken to the Medical Block. Oh, God, I shouldn't be here.*

Cupping his hands together a final time, and dipping them into the tub, he raised them up and let the warm water fall, rinsing the shampoo and any debris out. When he went through the motion a second time, her hands suddenly popped out of the water, and latched onto his.

You jerk, you're so fucking selfish, he thought, beginning an inner argument. *You're going to get her killed. But, she's not going to make it out of here, anyway. You can't save her, but you can save yourself, you can save your career. You're going to get caught. If you love her, you'll leave her. Get up, leave, go now. Before it's too late. Go. Now.*

She squeezed his hands, pulling them apart, and letting the water fall over her, placing them to her cheeks.

It took a minute, but Karl finally remembered to breathe. He stayed exactly where he was.

CHAPTER TWENTY EIGHT

"What was it you wanted to tell me?" asked Karl.

"What?" She dug her face into his warm hands still nestled against her cheeks.

"When we were on our way here tonight, you said there was something you wanted to tell me."

"Oh, right." She was quiet for a moment. "I want you to know that I do have feelings for Albert; he and I have known each other for a while, I've already told you that. I can't help how I feel about him—there is something there. But, I don't really know how deep it goes, and when I dream, I mean when I'm able to dream about anything other than this awful place, he's not the person I dream about.

"I'm so confused. I don't even know why I think about these kinds of things in a place like this. I should just be living, day to day, but there's someone here that makes me look forward to tomorrow. And, maybe those are dangerous thoughts in a camp. Then again, maybe, because I know there's no getting out, I want to feel anything I can, any human emotion, anything that reminds me that I am still alive, for the moment, still human. And, I think, that's why I feel certain things about someone other than Albert. About someone that I can physically touch, and can touch me back. I know I'm rambling…what I'm trying to say is that…I've come to feel something for you, too."

Karl's pulse raced, his heart feeling like it was going to burst out of his chest. He felt lightheaded.

"I didn't expect it," she continued. "Especially given what's changed in me for your brother since we got here. And, seeing how you and I met. But, I've come to feel something for you, for the person you've become, the change you've been making, and I can now look past that uniform."

"I need to tell you something, too," said Karl. "A confession." He struggled to focus his thoughts to make coherent sentences. "Though, I'm pretty sure that what I have to say has been obvious for some time."

"Say it, anyway. Please, say it."

"I have feelings for you, too. I try to stay away, I try not to think about you, but I can't stop. I just can't stop myself. No matter what I do, even setting you and Albert up on that date. Don't get me wrong, part of that was genuine, but I was also trying to get you out of my mind. Clearly, it didn't work. I think it actually made it worse, made me…jealous."

"I know that you can't seem to forgive yourself," she said, "for what happened that first night, in the shower, even though I have. I can see that in your eyes when you look at me. That's another reason why I've fallen for you. I know you're genuinely sorry for that. But, I'm scared, Karl. Not scared that you're going to do that again, but," she struggled, "afraid that maybe you won't want to touch me, now. I'm so scared to have any feelings at all, for anyone. But, in spite of how we met, I now feel safe with you. I know I'm not going to make it out of here. But, maybe that's why I'm going to do what I'm about to do."

"I don't understand," he said. "What are you going to do?"

"Hand me the towel."

He did as she requested, and watched her stand, as he remained kneeling. Water droplets cascaded down as she dabbed her thin, beautiful frame, here and there, until there was just enough moisture on her skin that she glistened, her nude body dancing, without moving, in the warm, flickering light of the lamp.

Still, Karl could see that she was shy, self-conscious of all the weight she'd lost since her arrival in the camp. She held the towel in front of her until he reached up and gently tugged on it, asking her, without speaking, to lower it.

She ran her hand over her head, across her short hair that used to be so long. He could see that she was beginning to lose herself in her own thoughts about her appearance.

"You're so beautiful," he said.

Else smiled and spread the towel out on the floor, and turned, still in the tub, to face Karl, pulling him up from his knees. She began undressing him. He quickly took over unbuttoning his shirt, allowing her hands to move lower, to his pants.

Holding his crumpled Nazi uniform in her hands, she started to toss it somewhere into the dark, when Karl took it from her, and laid it out, neatly, over the towel. She gave him an odd look.

"Can you think of a better way for two Jews to desecrate it?" he asked.

She shook her head, stepped out of the tub, and laid down on top of his clothes. Karl followed.

Twenty minutes later, as Else held him in her arms, their nude bodies still entwined, Karl thought to himself about what had just happened.

That's it, there's no turning back now. I'm a Jew, who has fallen in love with a Jew, and has now made love to a Jew. And, for the first time in my life, I'm happy.

CHAPTER TWENTY NINE

The following day, Karl lay in his bed, staring at the ceiling. All he wanted to do on his day off was lay there, and think about Else. How her soft, warm, wet skin felt next to his; how she felt on the inside. The thought of having to accept any visitors was the last thing on his mind; he didn't want anything, or anyone, to distract him from Else. Unfortunately, he knew that when a set of footsteps stopped outside his room, what he wanted no longer mattered.

"Karl?" A voice came from the other side of his closed door, followed by several knocks. "You there?"

Karl kept quiet, knowing it was Klaus, hoping he'd go away. The doorknob turned.

Damn, he thought, sighing. *Why don't they put fucking locks on those things?*

"Karl? You in here?" Klaus poked his head through the slightly open door.

"What do you want?" Karl asked. "I'm busy."

"Doing what?" Klaus swung the door open wide, and entered, followed by Hans and Wilhelm.

"Something other than listening to you three. Don't you guys have anything better to do than to keep harassing me all the time?"

"Wow. You know, you've turned into a real ass lately. I guess that's what happens when you get a promotion long before others, huh? You leave all us little people behind."

"What are you talking about?"

"You know," said Klaus, "your promotion and move out of here."

"No, I *don't* know, and do I really have to keep asking?" Karl sat up in his bed. "What promotion? And, what do you mean I'm being moved out of here? If all this is true, how do you know about any of it before I do?"

"Well, I'm not really surprised that you don't know. You do all these things that get the attention of our superiors, beating and killing Jews, I mean, but you don't have anything to do with anyone. Except, of course, your Jews. As far as me knowing before you, I have connections just like you do."

Karl grew more agitated and tired of Klaus' game. He lay back on his bed, again.

"You're being promoted to SS-Oberschutze, which really isn't such a big deal. No, the really big deal is that you're being shuttled out of here, going to the big time. Seems you impressed those visiting dignitaries so much, they want you near them."

"You're going to Berlin!" shouted Wilhelm. "You're going to work with the Fuhrer!"

Karl shot up, nearly jumping out of the bed. "The Fuhrer? Berlin? What the hell for?"

"You're not really going to work with Hitler," Klaus said, rolling his eyes. "Don't pay any attention to Wilhelm, he doesn't know anything. As far as why you're going to Berlin, beats me. Maybe they want you to make a film to teach all us idiots how to be real Nazis. Since you know how to do it better than anyone else."

"I don't know what you're mad about," said Karl. "I'm not the one that went looking into your background, like some spy, working for the Gestapo."

"Do you have something against our Gestapo?" asked Karl, squinting.

"No, of course, not." Karl backed down. Sure, he had connections, mostly his father and his apparent fans from the tour group, but Klaus' connections were far more secretive.

"Okay, fine, I get it," Klaus said. "I shouldn't have done that. I know there's no possible way you're related to that Jew. It's just so odd that you two look so much alike. But, see, that's where we, your friends, got so upset—you choosing those…things over us. You've spent more time with those parasites than with your German brothers…and, one particular sister. Claudia really likes you, and if you'd just give her a chance, you'd see she's got a lot to offer. Hell, you can just look at her and see that."

Karl remained silent, reclining again, looking up at the ceiling.

"He's kind of right," said Hans. "I mean, not about Claudia…I mean, he is right about her, that she is very good looking, but it's like you've chosen Jews,

The Camp

those lower than us, over pure Germans. The four of us met in boot camp, and we've been together since, all of us being assigned to this camp."

"You don't need to remind me," said Karl.

"Well, it sure as hell seems like we do," Klaus said.

"And, if you guys like Claudia so much, why don't you go out with her? You have my permission."

"She doesn't like us," said Wilhelm.

"She's been asking about you, wanting to know where you've been, but none of us have seen you for a week. We've all wondered where you are. What are we supposed to tell her?"

Karl didn't say anything, only rolling over on his side, facing the window, turning his back to the three guards.

"Look," Klaus continued, "here you are, about to be sent out, leaving us behind, but, it's like you really left months ago—when *he* came here. And now that you know that you're leaving, what are you doing? Still lying in that damn bed."

"Again, you're the one that dressed the Jew up, in *my* uniform, putting *my* career at risk, just for kicks. Or, did you casually forget about that?"

"Yeah, you're right, I did that, and the old Karl would have been just fine with it. He may have even been the one to come up with the idea. You may be some big shot with all those in charge, but I know that these fleas you've been hanging out with have done something to you. And, honestly, I'm glad you're leaving. You need to get as far away from them as possible, so that maybe you'll get out from under their spell. We sure as hell can't get through to you."

"You shouldn't have gone messing with my property, or my past. Sometimes, people change, but you're not one of those people."

"Change? Why would I need to change? There's nothing wrong with who I am. Are you listening to yourself? What are you saying? Are you a Jew sympathizer, now?"

"No!" said Karl, rising quickly to his feet, eyes locked onto Klaus'. He had to tread lightly now; be more careful with his words. "But, what I am is adaptable, and smart. You ask if I'm a Jew sympathizer, but who is it that's getting the commendations, the promotion, all the attention, being moved to Berlin, to the 'big time,' as Wilhelm put it? All you think about is the day to day killing, but you haven't stopped to think if there's a better way to do things. I've gained the Jews' *trust*, and that, my former friend, is more powerful than fear."

"*Former* friend?" Klaus repeated. "Now, what are you saying?"

"You're not stupid. Not completely. Figure it out."

"You little shit!" Klaus stormed across the room toward Karl, only to be held back by Hans and Wilhelm. "You really have chosen those fucking Jews over us. I can't wait until you're gone!"

Hans and Wilhelm pulled the struggling Klaus back toward the door, and out into the hall. Hans shut the door behind them.

Karl, his eyes closed, finally alone with his swirling thoughts and feelings again, began to panic. His heart raced adrenaline throughout his body. He lay back down and rolled on his side again, facing the window once more.

Fuck. Shit. I'm being moved to Berlin. Damnit. If I'm not here, I can't protect them. And no one else is going to do it. Fuck. One step forward, and ten fucking steps back.

Karl's eyes burst open when he heard clicking footsteps approach—women's heels. His door creaked open without a knock.

"I already know you're in here," said Claudia. "Klaus said that maybe I could get through to you. He was still yelling when Hans and Wilhelm got him outside. What happened?"

"I don't know." Karl rolled his eyes, and shut them tight, trying not to inhale. "Ugh, what is that smell?"

"It's a new Elizabeth Arden. Very fashionable. Helps keep the Jew smell off of me."

"I don't think you have to worry about anyone coming near you at the moment," he whispered.

"What?"

"Nothing. Look, you can stop right there. I'm not interested."

"Why is that?" she asked. "Why is it that I could probably have any man in this camp, except for the one that I actually want?"

"What does it matter? I'm leaving soon anyway, so I won't even be here."

"I know you're leaving," said Claudia, stepping closer to Karl's bed. "We could get married; I could leave here with you. I would make a great wife. We could climb the Party's social ladder, together."

"Married? You don't even know me."

The Camp

"Because you won't let me. Listen to me very carefully, Karl. I'm used to getting what I want. I haven't seen you in a week, but you plainly see that I'm not giving up that easily. Your friends seem to think that you are under some Jewish spell. All I can say is…that spell will soon be broken."

"What do you mean?" He finally rolled over from the window, to face her.

"You'll see. Then I'm going to put in for a transfer—to Berlin." She bent down toward him. "No one else will have you."

Claudia turned to leave, her blonde ponytail swinging around to follow.

"Claudia, I have to ask—why me? I mean, I don't even look like the kind of German a woman like you should be after. Klaus has blond hair and blue eyes, and I don't."

She stopped with the door open, turning her head to the side just enough to answer his question before leaving, a sly smirk peeking out. "Neither does the man who now controls most of Europe."

CHAPTER THIRTY

"Come in, Engel," said the SS officer from the other side of the office door.

"You wanted to see me, sir?" Karl's day off was growing ever more persistently less like what it was supposed to be—time to relax and think about Else.

"I do. Please, have a seat." The gray-haired officer remained in his chair, smoke rolling up from a fat cigar resting in a glass ashtray on his oak desk. "Herr Kommandant is out of the camp for the day, but he wanted me to give you the great news."

"Is it about my promotion and move to Berlin?"

"Why, yes, it is. How did you know?" the officer asked, his face wrinkled from curiosity, then, just as quickly relaxed. "Nevermind. I sometimes forget. It's a big camp, but one which is its own self-contained world. It gets smaller and smaller the longer you're here. And, people do like to talk. Spoils moments like this for the rest of us.

"Anyway, yes, you are being promoted and sent to Berlin. Your presence has been requested there by the very man whom you impressed so fully on his recent visit. Killing four Jews in the place of one, I believe it was? Brilliant move, Engel. I wish we had some coming in that were more like you, but it's not what I hear. But, anyway, congratulations are in order."

The officer stood, followed by Karl, and shook the young Nazi's hand. Each sat back down.

"Thank you, sir. If I may ask, what will be my new assignment, and when is the move to take place?"

"Well, let's see," said the officer, flipping through some notes on his desk. "Tomorrow is the first of April, so I do believe, in two weeks. Yes, the middle of the month is when you'll go. And, it looks like you're being reassigned to the administrative office of the Inspector of Concentration Camps."

"Actually, sir," Karl began, watching the fat Nazi on the other side of the desk puff away on the big cigar, "I was wondering if I may refuse the transfer."

The large man coughed and wheezed, turning green after having inhaled the cigar smoke upon hearing Karl's unusual request. He beat on his chest. "What?" he gagged.

Karl, feeling the urge to now piss his own pants, the same way Albert had that day in the barracks, could only think of Else, and his family, and doing what he could to stay and protect them.

"This is a very prestigious assignment," said the officer, "very cushy… easy. You would be in a position to mingle and rub elbows with those with real power, people who can really make a career for you. I've never even heard of someone trying to turn down an assignment like this. Even if you could refuse it, which you can't, you'd be a fool to do so. Why would you make this request?"

"I feel that my talents can best serve the Fuhrer here, in the camp."

Karl collapsed inwardly as the officer squinted at him through the still roiling smoke, as if he were a human lie detector, looking straight into Karl's soul.

"Bullshit, Engel. I wonder, and worry, if it's possibly connected to another issue about which I was to speak with you."

"Yes, sir?" Karl wondered if the officer could see him shaking.

"The Jews that you have been keeping such close company with."

Karl wanted to vomit, but held it in, praying that his face had not belied his intense surprise that someone else, in such high authority, knew what he'd been doing. He suddenly felt claustrophobic, the walls and furniture seeming to close in on him. The real question was: *how much* did the officer know?

"Yes, sir?" Karl repeated.

"We've known about the one that looks like you for some time, and your, shall we say, preoccupation with him. You look a little surprised. Don't be. We are Nazis. And, as I said, people do like to talk—that goes both ways. Your friends have been quite worried about you, afraid for your safety in such close proximity to the same Jews on a regular basis, which is understandable, given the powers they possess.

"Now, we've tried to keep our distance from what you do, since you have proven yourself fully capable of dispensing with the vermin that reside in this facility. But, after what happened between you and the other guard this morning, the Kommandant felt it necessary that a conversation take place, between you and I, in his absence."

Now, Karl wanted to go on a rampage, targeting specifically his 'friends.'

"Sir, forgive me, but they are not my friends. I have been betrayed by one in particular who called Berlin in order to confirm my parentage, to make sure that I wasn't Jewish because one of our prisoners looks so much like me. Could you not reassign him, instead?"

"No, we will not be transferring that guard. You were the one that was requested, you are the one that will go. And, you were not betrayed. He came to us with a legitimate concern, a suspicion, stated his case, and we authorized the phone call, to make sure that you were not a Jew. For you to call it a betrayal makes it all about you. It is not about you. It is about the integrity of the Party, the camp, the uniform you wear, and all that those things stand for. Besides, your friend was being exactly that—a good friend. If you had been found to be a Jew, then we would have reunited you with your family, right away."

The officer's sense of humor was as deadpan as one could get.

"Now, while we know that your interest in these particular rats lies purely in a scientific arena," the officer continued, "since there is no possible connection between you and the prisoner, we also worry that you may be giving them false hope. That they may think, as if thinking were even possible for them, or even hope, that they were somehow going to survive. And, while we appreciate the psychological impact that such thoughts have on an individual once they realize it was all a ruse, we nonetheless do not want any difficulties when it comes time to poison the rats. We like things to run smoothly. Do you understand?"

"Yes, sir."

"Very good, Engel. Your request to deny transfer is, in itself, denied. You will go to Berlin. Do you understand?"

"Yes, sir."

"Good. Now, as you may, or may not, be aware, there have been numerous attempts in the past several months at uprisings in a particular ghetto. Were you aware?"

"No, sir."

"Well, we have decided that we will, in response to these feeble attempts to rise against us, perform a mass extermination, larger than usual, on their holy day of…what's it called?" He rummaged again through his papers. "Ah, yes, Passover. This is to begin on the twentieth of April. Of course, you will not be here, as you will have already been transferred to your new assignment in Berlin.

"Now, none of this really has anything to do with you, but we wanted you to know that you will no longer need to provide that false hope to your particular Jews, as they will be among those that are executed that day. They have been kept alive long enough, and there will no longer be any use for them once you are gone. Death will not pass them over that day."

"I understand, sir."

"We, that is, the Kommandant and I, knew that you would. A young man such as yourself, of such proud parentage and birth, would have no problem in comprehending such matters. You know, no one has ever been promoted so quickly in this camp. We are very proud to say that you are one of ours. Herr Kommandant speaks very highly of you everywhere he goes. In fact, do not be surprised if the Fuhrer himself were to request your presence someday."

"That would, indeed, be a day to remember, sir."

"Very well, Engel. Well, that concludes our conversation. I do hope that you enjoy the rest of your day off. You may be excused, and, again, congratulations."

The officer again stood, shaking Karl's hand.

"Thank you, sir."

"Heil, Hitler," said the officer, snapping himself to attention, presenting the Nazi salute.

"Heil, Hitler," said Karl, following suit, then turning and leaving the room.

CHAPTER THIRTY ONE

Karl stormed into the Sonderkommando barracks, hours after meeting with his superior, and jerked Albert up from his bed by his ever-thinning arm, near-dragging him out of the building. Getting outside, into the darkest shadows of the night, Karl threw his brother against the side of the wooden structure, pinning him to the wall.

"Do you love her?" Karl asked, struggling to keep his voice to a whisper.

"I…I don't understand."

"You do—brother. You do understand. Do you love her? Do you love Else?"

"I haven't seen you since I was forced by your friends to kill that woman, a pregnant woman, Jewish or not; you haven't come by to check on me, to see how I'm doing, to see what killing a person does to someone, and this is what you want to talk about? Why didn't you stop it that day? Stop your friends from making me dress like that and killing her? Why didn't you stop that Nazi woman from killing the baby?"

"I know what killing a person does to someone," said Karl. "It breaks you and hardens you. And, they're not my friends…not anymore. I'm very sorry you were put in that position. You have to believe that there was nothing that I could do, not with Klaus there. And, now, I've learned that Claudia, the Nazi woman, is just a female version of him. Believe me, if I had tried to stop it, things would have been worse, for the both of us. You have no idea how bothered I was by it, but like I said, all the killing that you witness as a Nazi, it hardens you…makes you inhuman. You learn to turn your emotions off."

"Why do you want to know if I love Else? What business is it of yours?"

"I'm sorry I haven't come by," said Karl. "I've been busy. But, I need to know how you feel about her."

"I bet you've been busy. I know you've been visiting her, over there in family camp. I hear the guards here talk about things, while I'm shutting people in to be killed, moving their dead bodies to the ovens."

"You're right. I've been visiting her, and I've been busy being wrapped up in myself."

Albert backed down.

"I'm sorry, but I have to ask you again, do you love Else?"

"I've always loved her. So what?"

Karl backed away, turning his head, staying in the shadows.

"But, I don't understand," Albert continued, "what that has to do with anything. Has she said something?"

"If you've always loved her, why haven't you told her?"

"I was the son of a baker. I had nothing to offer her. Nothing."

"You had yourself. You had your love. That's all she's ever wanted. You could have tried."

"Well, I didn't. What does any of this have to do with anything? What's going on?"

"She has feelings for you, brother. She told me."

Karl lifted his head toward Albert's face, in time to see the kind of joy that only love could bring in a place like the camp.

"You should not have let her come here," said Karl. "You should not have allowed any of them, including yourself, to be brought to this place."

"What could I have done?"

"Gotten them all out of Germany, out of Poland."

"Impossible. I am not as strong as you. I'm weak, I always have been. I've never been very confident."

Karl rushed upon Albert, sending his twin reeling back again. The guard stood toe to toe with the prisoner.

"You helped our father run his business, practically shouldering it yourself. You were able to stay alive in the ghetto, and survived my attack on you, even attacking me after your date with Else. You've not committed suicide like so many other Sonderkommandos. And, you did all of this while I gained power from killing our own people. You have a strength of which you are not aware."

Karl again backed away, giving Albert space.

"I knew how you felt about her, without even asking you tonight," continued Karl. "Believe me, I felt it the other night when you shoved me. You attacked me, when you had no strength to do so. Only love would cause a man to do that." He took a deep breath, and let it out. "Would you have done things differently, gotten them out of the country if you had known about what was waiting for you here? If you had known about the camps?"

"No one knew about the camps. There were rumors, but no one really knew for sure. Besides, it would have been impossible to get them out."

"I am a Jew," began Karl, straightening his posture, "pretending to be a Nazi, who has yet to be discovered. Nothing is impossible." He backed away. "I ask you—you say you love Else, so what would you give to protect her?"

"My life."

"Thank you. That's all I needed to know."

"Why are you asking all this?" Albert asked.

"Something's coming."

Karl took Albert by the arm, this time with a much softer touch, and led him back toward the barracks door.

"I'm sorry, Albert," he said. "For everything."

CHAPTER THIRTY TWO

"You want to do what?" asked Miriam, sitting on her bunk in her now off-white, dirty dress.

"I want to help you celebrate Passover," Karl said. "I know it's an extremely important holiday to Jews; actually that's really all I know about it. Well, that and that you need to celebrate it that day."

Karl tried desperately to keep his voice down, yet still be heard by Miriam, though he found it difficult to do both, with children running up and down the housing's aisles, now that the Nazis were beginning to assign more and more families to the barracks on this side of the camp.

"I appreciate that, son, but it's just too risky for you. If we're caught—if you're caught—what would happen to you? You risk way too much as it is. I've been over that with you."

"The consequences of being caught in that act, on that day, is of such little concern, you have no idea."

"What does any of that mean? What's so important about that day, other than the Jewish holiday side of it?"

"Nothing that you need to worry about. When does Passover begin?"

"At sunset."

"Sunset?" Karl shook his head. "That won't work. We'll have to do it earlier that day."

"Earlier?" She stood up. "We can't start Passover before sunset. Why does it need to be earlier?"

"Something's happening that day, and I won't be available that evening. I'd also like to celebrate it with you, though I'm really not sure what's involved, what I need to do, what I need to provide. I don't know anything. I don't know anything about your God."

"You want to celebrate it with us?" Miriam's eyes welled. "You don't know how much that means to me. I know you've been working hard, going through a lot of changes. Else's been telling me all about it. Well, Karl, the first thing you need to know is that we have the same God as you were already raised to believe in. I know it's all very confusing for you, finding out you're Jewish, when you were raised as a Christian. Although, you were given a twisted version of what Christianity means by your parents when you were raised to hate. But, don't worry about the rest; I'll let you know what we need, if you really think we can get away with it."

"It's an important day, right?"

"Very."

"Don't worry about whether we can get away with it. Just get me a list of what's needed, as little as possible if you can, as soon as you can."

"I still don't understand the immediacy, or why it has to be before sunset. It's extremely important that it begin at sunset."

Karl looked around, making sure Else and Sarah were nowhere in sight, and sat Miriam back down.

"We're running out of time," he said. "You are running out of time. I am to be promoted and transferred to a post in Berlin. I tried to get out of it, but I can't. I won't be here to protect you any longer."

Miriam began to tear up again.

"That's not all," he continued. "Those in charge, in retaliation for ghetto uprisings, have scheduled a mass extermination that day, and you, Sarah, Albert, and Else, are to be included. They've chosen Passover on purpose."

Miriam trembled.

"Now, I am to be moved out of the camp before that day, but I will be back, to make sure that you are able to do what you need for Passover. I only know a couple of things about the holiday, like, it's supposed to last a week, but you're not going to have that. And, I think the day has something to do with celebrating a journey, freedom from bondage, or something like that, right?"

"Yes. I thought you said you didn't know anything about it." She tried to smile.

"So, with what's supposed to take place that day, you guys need to prepare for…the journey you will make, being set free from this place." Karl put his hand on his mother's shaking knee. "Your suffering will end. But, we have to do it before sunrise. It's the only chance you're going to have, because they'll start early that morning, so that they can accommodate all the people they want to kill."

"Sarah," whispered Miriam, wiping her tears. "Albert."

"Albert will be with you. I will make sure of it. All of us will be together for this Passover thing, to prepare for what's coming."

Miriam cried hard. Karl tried to shield her from the children who had begun to stop and stare at the crying woman.

"Just get me what you need as quickly as you can," he said, standing. "I'm sorry. I have to go, now. I have to begin preparing Albert."

"Okay," she sobbed. "Thank you, son. And, Karl, maybe I was wrong to tell you not to see Else. At least you will survive."

"Like you said, though, no one ever truly escapes the reach of a place like this. And, you're welcome…mother."

CHAPTER THIRTY THREE

1993

Karl paused his story when Agent Stein reentered the interrogation room. "Find anything?" asked Agent Williams, sitting in his chair.

"I did, sir," said Stein, eyeballing Karl. "Seems our elderly friend here, according to what we could find at the Holocaust Museum in D.C., has been lying the entire time." He handed a manila file-folder to the senior agent.

Williams opened the folder, flipping the papers inside, examining them closely. "Well," he began, "turns out the man that you claim survived, Albert Fogel, died, executed, at your camp, sometime in April of nineteen forty-three. So, both Albert Fogel, and Karl Engel, are dead. How do you explain that?"

"I think he had someone on the inside, another of his Nazi friends, hiding among Jews, fake the paperwork."

Karl arched an eyebrow. "Albert died on the twentieth of April, to be exact," he said. "All will be explained if you let me continue."

"So, you admit now that Albert died."

"That's correct."

"But, you said previously that he survived."

"Also, correct."

Williams threw the folder on the table, and stood, supporting his upper body on his hands as he leaned in toward Karl. "I'm getting tired of these mind games, sir. Which is it? Did Albert Fogel die, in the concentration camp, or was he saved?"

"Both, Agent Williams."

"Let's get him outta here, and just charge him, now," said Stein. "He's been stringing us along, just to fuck with us. He fucked with people then, and he's doing it now."

"Language, agent," said Williams, straightening his body, regaining his composure. "But, I do agree that it's all been a waste of our time." He turned to the elderly woman. "I'm very sorry, ma'am. I am completely at fault here for what you've had to endure over these past several hours. I'll have someone drive you home."

"Agent Williams," Karl said, "I have told the truth the entire time. If you do not let me finish, which it is time to do, the truth will come out later. At that point, if you allow me to be extradited overseas, the truth will come out on an international stage. You will be embarrassed, the FBI will be embarrassed, and I will bring a hefty lawsuit your way."

Williams, eyes squinted, stared at Karl.

"Sir, don't do it," said Stein. He leaned in to his superior. "Pull the plug on this guy, now. If you let this go on, he's right, you will be embarrassed, but only in front of the people watching from the other room."

"The other room?" Karl asked.

"The mirror, Mister Engel," said Williams. "It seems you've become quite the celebrity in the building and people have been gathering in the other room, on the other side of the mirror, listening to your story. More people than the room is made to hold. There's even a pot going as to whether you're telling the truth or not. At this moment, based on the information we've gathered, there's a small few in there that are collecting cash, as we speak."

"If you will allow me to continue, the tables will turn on them."

"We can't find any information to verify the existence of Sarah—no Sarah Fogel, no Sarah Engel, nothing."

"You don't think she'd have a married name? You think she'll be so easy to track down, in a couple of hours? It took fifty years for someone to find me. Don't worry about finding her—she'll find you."

"And how will I know even then that what you say will be the truth? How will I be able to verify it? According to this folder, Albert Fogel died in the camp. I don't know how you can convince me otherwise."

"Agent," said Aaron, Karl's son, "I understand your reservation. I've sat in here the entire time, and my faith in my father has been shaken, wondering if you've been right all along, thinking that maybe my father did commit those crimes, that maybe he actually is guilty. But, I'm going to see it through to the end—because I have to know. I *must* know where all this is going."

"Yes, son, I'm guilty. Everyone at that time is, or was, guilty. Guilty of killing, of not fighting back enough, of looking the other way, of letting it happen, of going along with it, of not doing enough to stop it when what was really going on was brought to light. Guilty."

Aaron looked to the floor.

"You're so close," continued the old man, staring at Williams. "You're only minutes away. You've come so far. Like my son said—see it to the end."

Williams looked at Stein, who shook his head, then at the elderly woman whose husband had been murdered all those years ago. She nodded. He looked at the mirror.

"Minutes, huh?" Williams asked.

"It's all about to come together."

"Finish it."

CHAPTER THIRTY FOUR

1943

"Here," said Karl, pulling a piece of bread from his right uniform pocket, "eat this."

"Thanks," Albert said. "But, I'm not hungry. Besides, I'm tired of eating treif food."

"Treif? What the hell is treif?"

"Non-kosher."

"Look, I've been taught why Jews are evil, a plague, and need to be wiped out, but I don't really know any of the truths about Jewish culture. So, please, stop your coded Jew talk and tell me what I need to know."

Albert rolled his eyes. "Kosher means that the food we eat has, or does *not* have, certain ingredients. It also means that it's actually prepared, meaning killed and cooked, according to specific standards."

"Wow. That's a tall order. Let me ask you, where do you think you are? What the hell do you think you've been eating all this time? We…I mean, they, the Nazis, are not going to go out of their way to give you treif, or kosher, or whatever the hell it is. Actually, if they're going to go out of their way to do something, it's to make sure something is *not* kosher. So, me being able to get kosher food is something that I will only be able to pull off one time, and that one time is coming, but it's not today."

The prisoner sat on his bed, as the guard stood next to him.

"Listen," said Karl, "I understand you're pissed off at me about a lot of things, but I'm about to try to pull off a miracle. So, would you rather be a good

Jew and not eat non-kosher food, and end up being a dead Jew, or do you want to eat any food and live?

"I understand that, as Sonderkommando, you go through more than the average prisoner. I understand that we lose more prisoners to that position, often without us touching them, than any other job in the camp. I understand that you've lost hope being here, you worry about our family, about Else.

"Now," Karl continued, drawing meat from his left pocket, "*you* need to understand a few things. You are going to start eating again. You need to put some weight back on, gaining your strength back, and you're going to eat whatever I bring you. You need to do this, as quickly as possible, because I've stopped eating. You've got about eighteen days to put a lot of meat back on your skinny bones. That's not a lot of time."

"Why do I need to do all this? Why are you on me about eating? Why have you stopped eating? What miracle?"

"You know, a lot of times you say you don't understand anything I'm talking about. Are you really so dimwitted, or is it an act?"

"I don't assume anything. I'm not going to jump to conclusions. I've learned to not think in this place, just do as I'm told, but, with you, I know I can ask the one word none of us are allowed to—why."

Karl took a deep breath. "Recently, Klaus and the other guards dressed you in my uniform, and I didn't see it immediately. Then, a few days ago, you said that you would give your life to save Else, to save our family. Well, you're not going to give your life—you're going to give mine."

Albert sat motionless, his mouth gaped open.

"Well," said Karl, "in a way, you'll be giving your life, but you'll still be the one walking out of here. To be more precise, Albert Fogel, the name, will die here, in this camp, in a little over two weeks, but someone's going to need to be carrying that name to their death for it to happen, and it won't be you—it'll be me in your place. If you do what I tell you, when I tell you to do it, you and the rest of our family, will be gone, away from this hell hole. I'm making arrangements now to have all of you moved underground and transported out of the country, though it's a little difficult at the moment, since those involved seem to not trust a Nazi making these requests."

"I don't under--."

The Camp

"I swear, Albert, if you finish that sentence the way you normally do, I'm going to lose my temper, and I can't have you walking around with cuts and bruises on your face, because I'm not about to get into a fight. All of this, the entire plan, all of their lives, hangs on you and your ability to adapt. You have to become me; you *must* become a Nazi. Or this…won't…work. Now, you'd better say you fucking understand, brother."

"Okay, okay," Albert said, standing, "I get it. I have to wear your uniform out of here, but, even though we argue a lot, and we really don't know each other, I don't understand why you have to die? Why can't we all go?"

"Because, Albert Fogel must die in a little over two weeks. Some people are going to make sure it happens. I'm being moved out of the camp before it happens, to a new position in Berlin, but I actually think it'll work to our advantage. All of you are scheduled to die, but I'll be back on that day, so we can make the switch, and the rest of you can leave. If Albert Fogel turns up missing, he will forever be hunted.

"Maybe, once in a while, a Jew escapes, but you won't have that luxury, not under your name. You'll have to use mine. Even then, it'll be dangerous because people from Berlin will wonder where I am, and come looking for me. It's a good plan, Albert, to get you out of the camp; it can work. Like I said, I'm working on getting you guys out of Europe, too, but I can't do everything. You have to do your part to get them out of here, and to the Allies."

Albert started crying. "We may have been split at birth, with you growing up as a Jew-hating Nazi asshole, and you may have nearly killed me, and tried what you did with Else, but, you are my brother. You've changed. I'm not having any part in this. You don't deserve to die."

"Then, you are dead; mom is dead; Sarah is dead; and, Else…Else is dead. All of you, and there isn't a damn thing I can do about it. These Nazis will win, when they could be beaten by a few Jews, but that's okay…they're the superior race, anyway."

Karl picked up the food from his brother's bed, and headed for the door, praying with each step.

"Wait," said Albert.

Karl stopped. Albert walked up behind him.

"How sure are you," began the man in the striped pajamas, "that it will work? What are the odds that we'll all be caught?"

"If we're caught, you will all die," Karl said, turning to face his brother. "And, I will die. They'll kill me for sure, and it'll be for nothing. If you don't try, you'll all die. If you trust me, and do what I say, I can get you all out. I'm betting my life on it."

"Karl, I--."

"Stop right there. Say nothing else. Now is not the time for that. We must get started immediately, and stay focused on what must be done. We can't afford any emotional attachment or sentimentality to get in the way; it could hamper the task at hand. Understand?"

"Yes."

"Okay, now, while you're eating, you need to listen very carefully to some things I'm going to tell you, information about me that you may need, things you may need to recite to prove you're me, in case you're ever questioned."

"Okay." Albert began picking apart the bread.

"I know I said you need to gain weight quickly, but keep in mind that your body has gotten used to not eating. Don't eat too fast; you'll get sick."

Albert slowed down, moving on to the meat.

"For the rest of your meal, I'm going to tell you every crime I've committed while working for these bastards. I'm going to tell you everything about my German parents, my childhood, my education, my training, all of it. I'm going to tell you about my relationships with Klaus, Hans, Wilhelm, and Claudia."

"Okay," Albert said, his mouth full of bread and meat. "Wait, who's Claudia?"

"Trouble. You met her the other day, when you were dressed in my uniform. There's more to her. I'm also going to tell you about my trips to family camp."

"I already know about those, remember?"

"There's more that you need to know, not information that's important to getting you out, but you just need to know."

"Like what? I mean, at first, I figured you were going over there, visiting mom and Sarah, but there was too much talk. Besides, I know nothing happened. Even if you had tried, Else would never do something like that."

Karl sat quiet. Albert stopped chewing.

"Nothing's happened, right?" Albert asked. "I mean, you two haven't done anything when you went over there, right?"

Karl watched a spark light in Albert's eyes, and it quickly dawned on him how to light his brother's fire.

"We'll talk more later." Karl whispered, again heading for the door. "I'll bring you more food, and I'll see you every day until they move me out of here. You've got a lot of work to do, and not long to do it in. We only have a couple of weeks for you to learn what would normally take months. Tomorrow, you learn how to be a Nazi."

CHAPTER THIRTY FIVE

"Come on, we've been at this for two days." Karl paced the line from one wall of the Sonderkommando barracks to the other, watching Albert, in his striped pajamas, walk. "How hard can it be to walk? If you can't even walk the way a Nazi would, you don't stand a chance. Forget everything else. This is the easiest part. Have you even been practicing?"

"The easiest part was the salute. And I practice when I can, but that's not often. The only times I'm really alone are when I'm with you. Can we please take a break?"

"A break?" A pacing Karl stopped. "You think the Nazis are going to give you a break if they figure out what we did when you're gone? It'll be a real English fox hunt. I'm about to be out of here, and won't be back for several days. I have to be sure that you can do this stuff without me."

Karl suddenly felt pity for his brother as he realized the enormous amount of pressure and weight resting on Albert's shoulders.

"Okay, let's take a break. Try on the uniform real fast, so I can see how much weight you've gained, before someone comes in here. We can talk about something else for a few minutes if you want."

Karl stared at the floor as he waited for Albert to change clothes.

"Have you thought about where you're going to take them, what you're going to do, when you get out of Nazi-occupied Europe?"

"Not really," answered Albert. "I've been so focused on what I'm supposed to be learning, and whether I *can* actually learn it in time, that I haven't really thought that far into the future. When you're a prisoner here, you learn not to think about the future."

"Well, you should give it some thought, just in case you do make it. I think you're right, you definitely need to concentrate on the task at hand, but it might also help to see yourself somewhere else, far away from here. What about America? They call it the land of opportunity."

"That's so far away. Besides, you're assuming that the Allies will win."

"How can an evil like this not be defeated?" asked Karl. "Anyway, America being so far way is my point. Maybe you could take Jakob's…our father's dream and open a bakery there. You have the knowledge and experience to do it."

"I don't know."

God, how do I get through to him? thought Karl as Albert finished getting dressed. *He's already given up.*

"Well, this uniform is still just hanging off you," said Karl. He pulled at the sleeves covering Albert's thin arms. "I can tell you're gaining weight, but not quickly enough." He stood back, thinking. "It's that damn job. You're working off so much of what you're putting on.

"Unless…you still need to add the weight, but instead of forcing my uniform size to fit you, what if I requested a smaller size, then put you in that? I am losing weight. They'll ask why I'm losing so much, and I'll say that…"

"You're nervous about the promotion to Berlin and making the camp, your parents, and the whole Nazi party, proud?"

"Well, son of a bitch," said Karl. "You *can* use that brain of yours when you want to. That's good. Yeah, that's what I'll say. But, you still need to eat more; you'll need the energy and strength.

"Still, that's not the only problem. You know the mechanics of the salute, but you still need to work on that, as well. The salute…the walk…what is it that you're missing? What am *I* missing?" Karl sat on the bed, his head in his hands.

"Let's face it, I can't do this. I'm not good enough."

Karl slowly raised his head. "That's it. That's fucking it. You lack the confidence of someone who truly *believes* they are superior to everyone else around them, let alone any other race or class of people. You gotta get that shit that you can't do it out of your head.

"When you're a Nazi, everyone, and I do mean *everyone*, is beneath you. It's not just the Nazis I'm talking about—*you* are the apex of civilization and God's creations. You have to *believe*, and *act*, like that is a universal truth. Along with that comes indifference to everyone else. On the day that we make the switch, and until you get to an Allied country, if you are ever encountered by Nazis, you gotta treat our family, and Else, like garbage."

"You ask so much of me."

"Because their survival, and yours, depends on it. If you love them, you will hate them, when you have to. At least, make it appear so."

"I know what I have to do, what I'm *supposed* to do, I just don't know that I *can* do it. I don't know that I can even *act* like a monster."

"Right now, you're weak, not just physically, but inside, too. Being on the Nazi side of the camp, I mean, as a Nazi, not a prisoner, I can only imagine how you feel. This place is designed to break you physically and mentally. Believe me, I know *exactly* what I'm talking about when it comes to the design of these places. And, they've succeeded in that goal—you are definitely broken. But, I also suspect that you lacked some confidence before you got here. You also don't have the indifference and the internal strength to do what must be done.

"No, if we tried to make the switch today, all of us would be dead, including me. So, you've got to find a way to put some of those broken pieces of yourself back together. I don't think you'll ever be truly whole again, not after being here for even a single day, and it's not going to help that, come a couple more weeks, by the time I'm finished, you *will* act like a monster. Actually, like I said, you'll have to go beyond acting…you'll have to *become* the monster. But, it will save your life. These guys will see through an act. And, I'll be damned if I'm going to sacrifice myself for nothing." Karl looked down at the floor. "Not that it matters…I'm damned anyway."

Albert walked over, laying his hand on his brother's shoulder. Karl shot up from the bed.

"We need to get back to work. Stay focused. If I can change in a few months after years of being in the dark, you can stand that darkness for a short time. Do the walk again. Remember, you are pure, superior, your Fuhrer walks on water, and you fucking *own* those Jews that are with you."

Karl drilled Albert, repeatedly, giving commands, as quietly as possible, like a training officer in boot camp. The Jewish Nazi teaching another Jew how to become a Nazi. Over and over they ran through it: the walk; the demeanor, and not just the Nazi way of carrying oneself, but also the way Karl does; a snappy, right-armed salute, coupled with a 'Heil, Hitler,' for good measure.

"You've got two weeks to make all of this second nature," said Karl. "I don't want you to focus on anything else. Even if you're not physically alone, I want you to be alone in your mind, going over this stuff in your head. And, remember, I, Karl Engel, would never hesitate to kill a Jew. You have to keep that in the back of your mind."

"I've already killed someone," said Albert, his voice dropping like a stone in water. "I'm not doing it again."

"You damn well will," Karl said, charging his brother, when, suddenly, he remembered two days earlier, when he brought up Else, then dropped the conversation. He remembered the jealous flame he saw in Albert's eyes. Karl stopped in his tracks. "I never did finish what I started talking about the other day."

"I remember," said Albert, almost whispering, his head hung low. "I was hoping you wouldn't bring it back up."

"I am bringing it back up."

"Please, don't do this."

"I love Else." Karl watched Albert's fists clinch. "That's right. I love her. I tried to get her out of my head, even set you up on that date of yours, but nothing I tried worked. Finally, she forgave me for that night in the shower, when we first met. You remember her telling you about it?"

Karl knew he was treading a thin line, risking everything, not fully knowing how Albert would react to being pushed in that direction, hearing Albert's breathing, and seeing his face redden from the increased blood flow. But, push he did.

"And, I'll tell you something else," he continued, "she loves me."

Albert looked at Karl as if the Devil himself stood between him and the woman he loved.

That's it, Karl thought. *Keep it coming.*

"But, there's one more thing," Karl said. Even he was now unsure about whether to continue, but knew he had to draw the anger, and the strength that would come with it, out. He backed up. "We made love about a week ago."

Albert rushed upon Karl, grabbing him by the throat, and throwing him to the cold, cement floor.

"That's it, become the emblem on your lapel," said Karl, referring to the Death's Head on the Totenkopfverbande uniform. "Become death."

Albert stopped, looking at his fist reared back, ready to strike.

"You see," said Karl, "everyone's got it in them. You just need to find their breaking point. And where you are right now, is where you need to stay, until you get them out of this country, out of all Nazi territory in Europe. I'm sorry, Albert, that you had to find out at all, but I did have to tell you."

"I know she loves you," Albert said, the shock on his face having not subsided in the least. He released Karl, and sat down. "Why did it have to be her, though? Why Else? You knew before the night that you…you knew how I felt about her."

"You're right, I did know. I told you, I tried to stay away, I really did, but I couldn't stop thinking about her. I fell in love with her, and I can't really apologize for that. It was one time, and it's not going to happen again. But, you are my brother, and I do apologize that I hurt you, and I know that means nothing, at this moment. I'm offering you a chance, though, to save her, to give her the life that I can't. If it means anything, she did tell me that she loves you, too."

"She said loves?"

Karl got on his feet, rubbing his neck. "She actually said she has feelings, but what's the difference? Hey, you're going to have to look beyond what happened between me and her, because you're the one that gets her, brother." He walked over to his brother, resting his hand, lightly on Albert's shoulder. "I needed to know that you can get her, all of them, to safety. That you can take care of…them, later. I'm not saying that I know what the future holds, but I do have hope that two people who care about each other can find their way, together, through all this darkness."

Albert sat quiet, for a few moments, until he finally got back up. "Let's run through it all again."

CHAPTER THIRTY SIX

"It'll never work," said Albert, turning around in Karl's gray, smaller-sized SS uniform.

"It'll work," responded Karl, closely examining his brother. "You've practiced everything we started a couple of weeks ago, everything I've taught, while I've been gone these past few days in Berlin, right? Everything ends tomorrow."

"Yes, I've practiced, but...does anyone know you're here?"

"Only the night guard at the front gate. I'm not worried about him; he doesn't pay attention to anything."

The resemblance in the uniform was now more remarkable than it was when Klaus had dressed up Albert. Albert had put on more weight, and this Nazi uniform fit the Jewish prisoner perfectly, from the cuffs stopping at the wrists, to the collar, with the Death's Head symbol, closing around his neck in a way that, as Goldilocks would say, was just right. Karl made sure that even the hat was the proper size.

And Karl, himself, had lost an incredible amount of weight since limiting his intake at the beginning of the month. The twins were now fairly even.

"It's mean," Albert continued.

"It's not mean." Karl paused. "Well, it's a little mean. But, it'll work. Look, if you can fool her, you can fool the idiot guards that work this place, well, most of them, for a few minutes. Just enough time to get our family out. Don't do anything stupid when you're with her; just talk to her."

"Wait, I'm confused. What do you mean *most* of the guards? Can I fool them or not? You said the guards would be able to see through an act, now you're saying that they're idiots."

"Okay, the only reason they catch on to anything is because of their paranoia. But, there are a couple of guards here that are more of a match for us than the others. Now, I've already covered them a little bit with you, but you need to make sure you understand what you're up against.

"Klaus definitely has it out for you; he even came really close to finding out the truth about me. He's smart, and we shouldn't underestimate him. Claudia is just as formidable, conniving. She may actually be the bigger problem. She's after me, in a romantic way. She's had her sights locked on me and won't let go. Fucking crazy, that woman is. If she thinks I'm still alive, I honestly think she'll try to find me, even if I have disappeared from my job in Berlin. If she figures out what we did, I'm confident that she will come after you, and she won't stop.

"If either one of them figure this out, though, they'll let the other know, and they may put the dogs on you, figuratively, and literally. Then again, they may not want any of their superiors to know about their embarrassing blunder, outwitted by a few Jews, and my hunt you down themselves. Either way, I don't want you to worry; they won't see this act coming, as long as you've been practicing."

"Oh, my God, we're all dead. Yes, I've been practicing. But…it won't work."

"Stop saying that." Karl pushed Albert toward the door. "Let's get through tonight, first. Do your best to not be nervous. You're used to keeping your eyes low; now, you have to keep you head high. Remember, you're a Nazi. Fool her, and the rest will fall into place. Look, if you get into any trouble on the way there or back, just salute and say 'Heil, Hitler.' That's all you need to do. And, give her this bag." He passed a small sack to Albert, and opened the barracks door. "Good luck."

Albert, trembling, stepped out into the dark light of the camp. Fifteen minutes later, he'd made it to family camp, having no trouble at all. No one questioned him. No salute or declaration of loyalty to the Fuhrer required.

Remembering the directions Karl gave him to find the women's barracks, Albert walked inside, like he owned the place, and pulled Else out the back of the building, at first taking a left turn, instead of a right, then quickly correcting himself, as he escorted her to the showers. He'd paid little attention to the path he and Karl had taken when he was there before, on his date.

"What's going on?" she asked, entering the building. "You okay?"

Albert stood, with his back to her, turning around slowly to bring his face into the moonlight shining through the open door. "I'm fine."

"You sure?" she moved closer, putting her hand to his cheek. "You're cold. And, clammy. Are you running a fever?"

"If you had to choose between me, me being Karl, and Albert, who would you choose?"

She only gave a look of bewilderment at his question.

"Nevermind, that wasn't fair," he said. "How do you feel about me?"

"What do you mean? You're acting strange. What's going on?"

Albert knew that Else was clearly aware of what he meant, the question was simple, but she seemed to want to dance around the topic, appearing to want to keep her true feelings at a distance from even herself.

Else leaned in to kiss him; Albert back away.

"I'm not supposed to do anything stupid," he said. "But, I want to hear you say it."

"What are you talking about? Karl, please tell me."

"Here, before I forget, I need to give you this." Albert handed the small bag given to him by Karl, to Else.

She opened it, pulling out a tiny amount of leavened bread, a feather, wooden spoon, candle, and a couple of matches.

"I don't know what to say, Karl. Thank you."

"Just make sure that when everyone looks for the chametz by candlelight tonight, the entire group gathers around the light so no one outside the barracks sees it."

"I will."

Else moved closer. "Is there something else? You seem distant."

"Do you love me?"

"Karl, I...I'm scared to say that I love you. I'm scared of the hope that comes with saying that word. Not hope that you would feel the same, I know you do, but hope in the future. I don't want to feel that in here, in this place."

Albert looked at the floor, out the door, back at Else, and moved in, kissing her. Else's lips were soft, softer than he dreamed they would be. He felt his breath draw out of him as she kissed him back, then rush back into his lungs when she stepped away.

"Oh, my God," she said.

"Please," he began, "don't be mad, at me or Karl. This was not a joke played on you. I just...I wanted to know what it was like to be my brother and be loved by you. Please, don't tell my mother. You say that you don't want to use the word love in a place like this, because of the hope that comes with saying such a thing."

"Oh, my God," she repeated, her fingertips pressed to her lips, shaking. "Albert," she whispered, tears falling down.

"Something I'm beginning to believe in, though, is that, even in here, until we reach our last moment of life, hope endures."

Albert walked out of the showers, back to Karl, harassed only by his own thoughts.

CHAPTER THIRTY SEVEN

20 April 1943

Karl and Albert moved silently through the camp on an early April morning, Passover, just before dawn. The clock was ticking before the mass gassing was to begin. The switch was only an hour away. All the time spent practicing, the rehearsal, the planning, it all came down to this day, this morning, this hour.

Albert suddenly spied a dark figure standing in the shadows of the entrance to family camp, a presence betrayed by the small red light of a lit cigarette. Karl let a small knapsack he'd been carrying on his shoulder slide down his arm, to his hand, hiding it behind him. The man in the shadows flicked the dead ashes from the lit cigarette, the glowing red tip burning brighter, as the guard and his prisoner approached.

"Where you going?" asked Klaus.

Albert noticed Karl scanning the area, no doubt looking for Wilhelm, Hans, or any other guards. There was no one.

"It's just me," Klaus continued. "Where you going?"

"What's it matter to you?" asked Karl.

"I guess it doesn't," said Klaus, shrugging his shoulders with a smirk. "Love your new hair, by the way." He reached out to touch Karl's newly-shaved head, causing a jerk-back reaction from Albert's brother. Klaus laughed. "And, you're looking a little thin these days. You want to look more like him, huh? I can't believe it—a Jew-loving Nazi. And, apparently, you've taken off work in Berlin to come back down here to what, hold his hand when he goes in? I was already disgusted by him, just for being Jewish, but then he came between me and you, destroying our friendship. But, you," Klaus shook the two fingers holding the lit cigarette at Karl, "you, disgust me even more, because you let it happen. But, it doesn't matter. As long as the Earth is cleansed of his filth."

"Soon enough," said Karl, "your Jew will be gassed, and anything that's left of our friendship will go up in smoke."

Klaus took a drag off his cigarette, blowing the smoke in Albert's face.

"Oh," Klaus said, moving closer to Albert, still speaking to Karl, "I know he will, because, I volunteered for the job, myself. I'm going to see him to the shower, lock him in, then climb on the roof and drop the Zyklon B pellets down the hole. Then, I'm gonna watch his body go in the oven—like a lamb.

"But, I also want you to know, Karl, that your Jew women are in good hands, too. Especially that Jew girl you've been so infatuated with. Claudia volunteered to come over and take care of them. She'll be here soon. She's also put in for a transfer to Berlin, and got it. Maybe now, once all this is over in a few minutes, you can move on, and we can all get back to normal. I'm willing to forgive you, Karl, since you were obviously under some kind of demonic hold."

"Well, thanks for the talk," said Karl, pulling Albert along. "I'm going to prepare your lamb, now, for the roast."

"Go ahead, Jew, go in the barracks and pray to whatever idol you call a god. I'll be out here, waiting." Klaus raised his voice, continuing to shout at Albert. "If you people are the chosen ones, where is your god now, Jew? Yeah, you've been chosen alright—chosen to die!"

Klaus walked toward the gate, and leaned against it, smoking his cigarette, waiting for the coming light of dawn and Albert's return.

Escorting his brother inside, Karl handed his knapsack to Miriam, who removed the matzo found near the top, then stood aghast as she reached her hand back in and pulled out a folded SS uniform.

"What is this?" she asked.

"Part of the plan," said Albert.

"What plan?" asked Miriam. "Why is your head shaven, Karl? Why are you so gaunt?"

Else approached Karl, grabbing him by the arm. "Why was Albert wearing your uniform last night? What was that all about? Some kind of game?"

"I'm sorry, Else." Karl said. "No, it was not a game. Look, we don't have much time." He turned to Miriam. "We need to do anything Passover related right now. We've got about forty-five minutes. If I'm not mistaken, we need to burn the yeast, I mean the, um…chametz. Sorry, I don't know how to pronounce it."

"It's okay," said Miriam.

All the Jews in the barracks gathered around Miriam who led the burning, the white smoke drifting to the ceiling.

"Okay," began Karl, "which of us is firstborn—me, or Albert?"

"You," smiled Miriam. "You've been studying."

"Yeah, Albert's not the only who's had homework. Now, everyone, we're going to have to do this differently than you normally would. Please, take a piece of matzo."

Karl passed the unleavened bread around, taking none for himself in order to observe the fast of the firstborn. He searched the group and found who looked to be the youngest girl present.

"How old are you?"

"Seven."

"I think this where you start asking the questions, right? Since, you're the youngest here."

"That's right," Sarah said. "We prepared her last night. Albert can translate for you, Karl, since you don't speak Hebrew."

"Mah Nishtana HaLeila HaZeh?" asked the seven-year-old.

"Why is this night different from all other nights?" whispered Albert.

"I'm sorry," Karl whispered back, "I couldn't get a Haggadah."

"It's okay. Like you said, this is not a normal Passover observance. You did what you could."

The minutes passed as all the Jewish women in the barracks, and Karl and Albert, celebrated the holiday to the best of their ability, a celebration brought to fruition by a Nazi.

Albert watched Else from time to time, noticing her eyes darting back and forth between the two brothers. She was clearly nervous…and curious.

Finally, the moment came for the ceremony to end, and the final journey to begin.

"Sarah, Albert, and Karl," began Miriam, "I want to quickly tell you three about your births." She took Sarah's hands in hers. "After the boys were born, your father and I desperately wanted a little girl. We tried and tried, but I kept miscarrying, until, finally, one stayed—you. We had some close calls, thinking I'd lost you, too, but it was like you were completely defiant. You were telling us that you weren't going anywhere.

"And, on the day you were born, yours was the easiest birth. It was the shortest. You, my angel, were the miracle we kept praying for. Your father was so happy that day, he didn't want to hand you over, even though he was afraid he'd drop you because of his hand." Miriam smiled through her tears. "We both loved you every second of your life."

Miriam let go of Sarah, and took a hand from Karl and Albert. "Jakob and I never thought we'd have twins." She stopped her story, the pain of giving up a child breaking through for all to see. Miriam squeezed her sons' hands. "All those moments I wish I could have back," she whispered. She cleared her throat. "That morning was so cold, still winter. Jakob was at the bakery when I went into labor and was taken to the hospital. A nurse ran all the way to your father's work to tell him. He had no one to cover the business, so she stayed, and when word got out what was happening, the neighborhood pulled together, and kept the store open so that he could make it. He, too, ran all the way, in the cold, forgetting his coat.

"But, he made it, just in time, to see you, Karl, come first. Then, a few minutes later, Albert, you followed your brother. I know I told you already, Karl, but you were so sick, and Albert, your cry was so strong. It was like one had given so much of their strength to the other." Miriam broke down. "And now, it's happened all over again."

Miriam stood, and pulled Albert and Karl aside. She raised Karl's uniform sleeve, revealing a tattooed copy of Albert's number.

"I know what you boys are up to," she said, her eyes tearing up. "I want you both to know how proud I am that you worked together on what you're going to do. Karl, as you've learned, Passover marks the night that all of the Egyptian first-born died, yet the Lord passed over the Jewish homes, all of which resulted in the release of the Jewish slavery. Thus began our exit from Egypt." She placed a hand to each one of her sons' cheeks. "Today's dawning light brings yet another Exodus."

Karl put his hand to hers. "It is today, in our darkest hour, when our light shall shine brightest."

"Yes, my son. Now, you both need to hear, that I will not be leaving this place as you have planned."

"What the hell are you talking about?" asked Karl. "Yes, you are."

"Mom, of course you're going," Albert said. "Now, get yourself together. We only have a few minutes."

"I'm sorry, boys," Miriam continued. "I can't do that. I'm too weak, and would only slow down you three that are going. It's going to be difficult enough for you, Albert, to get Sarah and Else out of Nazi territory. I can't physically do it. You both know I'm right. You know it. It gives the three that are leaving a better chance.

"I can't tell you how overcome with joy I am that I was able to see all of my children together, having lost one for eighteen years." She placed both hands on Karl's cheeks, rivers of tears moving down both faces. "I've said goodbye, in my head, to everyone, every morning, since I got here. Yet, I believe, that my time in this camp has turned out to be a miracle. I'm ready."

"Mom--," Albert began.

"No," she said. "You get Sarah and Else out of here. I know you can do it. You have to. I believe in you. No one else could have survived all of this, and learned what you have learned. You've found a strength you didn't know you had, but I knew."

"We can save you," said Karl, shaking.

"Oh, my sons, my beautiful boys." Miriam could barely finish the rest of her words. "My boys so beautiful that I had two of you. Karl, you saved me the moment I found you again."

"No, mom, you saved me when you gave me up, giving me a chance at life the only way you could. And, today, I'm going to give your other children a chance."

CHAPTER THIRTY EIGHT

Karl and Albert ran to the knapsack, the gray uniform lying on top. In a flurry of clothing, Albert removed his striped pajamas, passing them to his brother who then gave the smaller Nazi outfit to his twin. Karl helped Albert make sure the SS attire fit as neatly as possible. The prisoner uniform draped like a large sheet over Karl's now-malnourished body.

"What's going on?" asked Else, watching the two men. Albert saw her look to Miriam, who looked away. Suddenly, her expression belied her understanding of what was taking place. "No. This can't happen. You two can't do this. Why are you doing this?"

"We have a chance to get you and Sarah out," said Albert. "We're taking it."

"Why not all of us? What about your mom? What about Karl?"

No one answered.

"Karl's going, too, right?"

"Listen, Albert," Karl said, "I almost forgot. When you get out of the camp's gate, go left, and run into the forest. Stay low. You'll find a car hidden. You'll also find the spare tire on the hood is loose. Remove the tire, and you'll see a note underneath with instructions about what to do and where to go next. Don't forget to secure the tire back to the hood."

Karl stopped and ran over to a hole in the wooden wall of the barracks, when a commotion arose outside the barracks.

"What is it?" asked Albert.

"They're starting to round up Jews for the procession." Karl paused, listening again. "And, something happened during the night. Something about a ghetto, in Warsaw. I'm not sure." He peered out the hole. "The Jews are being moved faster than usual. Klaus is still standing there, waiting." Karl stood erect.

"Whatever's happening, it's working to our favor. All of the guards, except for him, seem distracted. Most are moving toward the gate."

"This is the best chance we're gonna get," said Albert. He noticed the larger group of women gathered in the barracks, huddled together, as they watched what was happening. None approached to ask him to take them, too—they were all waiting to die.

"Right." Karl took a deep breath. "It's time."

"No, please," said Else. She ran to Miriam. "Do something. Stop them. This is wrong."

"I am their mother," Miriam said, smiling through her tears, taking Else's hands. "No mother wants to see anything happen to their child. I lost one then found him again; he was not alone when he came into this world, and he won't be alone when he leaves it. For two of my children to live, this has to happen. I have to go, as well. For you to live, this has to happen. You'll be a mother someday, and you'll understand what it's like to feel so much love for your child that you would die for them. One of my son's is giving his life for you, and the other is getting you to safety. This is right."

"But…," Else turned in multiple directions, facing Albert, facing Karl, turning back to Miriam. "I feel…I'm so confused."

"There's nothing to be confused about," said Karl. "Get ready to move with Albert."

"It's okay, dear," Miriam said. "I know that you care for both of them, just as they both care for you. They are doing this because both love you."

"Yes," Else whispered, "I do care for both." She turned to Karl. "And, you think they're going to just let us walk out here?"

"That's right. Albert has fake papers, in his uniform, authorizing your transfer and transport, along with my identification. It's amazing how often people in administrative positions will sign anything that's put in front of them, especially in Berlin, because they don't take the time to read what it is they're signing. They just ask you what it is, you tell them, and they put their names on it. So, someone in Camp Administration thinks they signed papers authorizing the building of another crematorium."

Karl, in his striped pajamas, seeming to wait for Else to offer one final embrace, finally walked over to Sarah, and knelt. He kissed her, hugged her,

The Camp

crying hard. Sarah trembled. Karl stood, hugged Albert, and whispered in his ear, sending Albert into a fit of tears. Karl headed for the barracks door.

Miriam embraced her daughter, saying nothing. Sarah shook violently, clutching her mother's dress. Miriam let go and hugged Albert, again without speaking. The matriarch joined Karl at the precipice.

"I'm going with you," said Else, running to the door.

"No, you're not," Karl said, shooting a look to Albert who pulled the young woman back. "You have to get Else and Sarah out now, brother, before Claudia comes to collect them. She'll be here any minute."

"All of us can help distract the guards," said one of the elder women approaching from the larger group.

"Thank you," Albert said. "I...I wish there was something I could do to get everyone out. If we had a way to get more--."

"You would never be able to do that," interrupted the woman, "but, if you can get your two women out, then generations will continue."

"No!" yelled Else. "I don't want to leave! I don't want to live! I want to die!"

"Then my son's sacrifice will be for less than it is meant to be," Miriam said. "He will be saving my other children, but you are another life that can be saved by his. You are not meant to die here today."

"Else," said Albert, in a low whisper, holding her from behind. "I love you. I need you. I can't do this without you. You have to leave with me and Sarah."

Else collapsed to the floor.

"You once told me," began Karl, kneeling beside her, "that life is about making choices. Right now, you have to choose life." He pulled her to her feet. "Life...Else."

She pulled a piece of paper from her dress pocket, and handed it to Karl. Albert watched his brother unfold it, and saw that it was a drawing, made with coal, of her and Karl at the camp, holding hands.

"Karl...I love you," said Else.

"And, I love you. Always."

Karl refolded the drawing, put it in his armpit, and kissed Else on her wet cheek. He walked to the still closed door, beside his mother, opened it, and held Miriam's hand as he escorted her toward Klaus. The German, still waiting at the family camp gate, smiled as they approached.

Albert, Else, and Sarah, stood in the shadows as the rest of the Jewish women followed out the door, the greater community masking the presence of the remaining three.

Albert watched as Klaus spoke to his brother, then knocked him to the ground, laughing. The Nazi yanked Karl up and pushed the Jew and his mother in front of the line, toward the gas chamber. The plan worked.

CHAPTER THIRTY NINE

1993

"I never saw my brother, or mother, again," said Karl Engel, having now revealed his true identity to be Albert Fogel, while rolling up his sleeve to show his tattooed number. "Albert and Miriam Fogel died that day, executed, in the camp.

"Son, I know you've been wondering all this time why you were never told about your Aunt Sarah, though she knows about you. We kept in touch over the years through a post office box, sending pictures and letters. But, we haven't actually seen each other in a long, long time. Much of it revolves around an incident that occurred when we were escaping Europe. Some things are much too difficult to forgive."

Karl drifted away, in his mind, until he suddenly snapped out of it, and looked around the room.

"Anyway, you were not told about Sarah, not just because of what happened between her and me, but also because I felt that I had to keep everything, including her, a secret for your protection. I didn't want you asking too many questions about our past, or say the wrong thing to the wrong person about who we really were, since we were trying to keep a low profile. I realize now that the lies, my omissions, were only damaging and not protective at all. I'm sorry."

Everyone in the room stayed silent for several minutes, until Agent Stein finally broke the quiet.

"And, you," he began, looking at Aaron, "you really never knew any of this? Never saw the tattoo?"

"No. I'm as shocked as everyone else. My mother never mentioned it. As far as the number goes, dad has always worn long sleeves, saying his skin is especially sensitive to light. I had no reason not to believe him. He's my father."

"What about when you went swimming?" asked Agent Williams.

"I never learned to swim. The only person who knew the truth was, obviously, my wife, Else. We were married not long after leaving the camp. I always knew that she loved me, and I loved her, but there was also a part of her that she kept hidden, though I knew what it was—she harbored a love for my brother, Karl, until the day she died, about six months ago. She never spoke about him, and I never brought him up. But, anytime she would hear someone speak my name, my assumed name, she grew distant in her eyes.

"I know she loved me, mostly because, she just did, that's how love is, but also because of the life I provided for her. She loved my brother, though, because he *gave* her life. She saved him, too, though. I was always a good person, I like to think, but another reason Else loved Karl so much was because he found his humanity through her. Her forgiveness and love for him was his true redemption."

He cleared his throat before continuing, fighting back tears. "And Aaron, as far as me being your father, I don't really know who your true father is. Your mom never said, and we never talked about it. Of course, it's impossible to go by looks, since my brother and I were twins, and you look like your mother, anyway."

"But, why keep the name Karl Engel?" asked Williams. "Once you made it to America, why not go back to being Albert Fogel? I mean, to keep using a German name, at that time, couldn't have gone well. I would think that going by a Jewish name would have been better. Actually, I don't know what to call you now."

"You asked me when this all began if my name was Karl Engel, and I said, 'yes.' That hasn't changed. So, you may call me Mister Engel, or Karl, if you prefer. I found when I got to this country, that no matter which name I used, German or Jewish, it wasn't going to be easy. I feared reprisals from Americans, Nazis, and Nazi hunters. So, there was really only one reason why I never changed my name—my brother gave his life to save a family, and I wanted to restore some good to his name. Albert Fogel died in the camp, but Karl Engel lived on, through me, and each time I did some good work, a little bit more of the bloodstain that came with his name was removed."

CHAPTER FORTY

The elderly woman in the interrogation room got up from her green leather chair, walked around the table, and hugged Karl.

"I'm sorry," she whispered, her German accent dripping from her tongue. "Please forgive me."

"There is nothing to forgive," said Karl. "No one was ever supposed to know."

"We have both suffered for fifty years. Please, let me wipe a little more of that stain away—I forgive your brother."

She ran her wrinkled hand across Karl's face, as he grabbed hold of it, sobbing, and kept it in place.

"Sir," said another dark-suited agent, poking his head into the room, "there's a call for you."

"Just a moment. Ma'am," said Agent Williams, his hand extended to usher the old woman out, "it's time to go, now. Agent Stein, will you step out with me?"

"Of course, sir."

The two FBI agents, and the old woman, exited the room, leaving Karl and his son to talk. The father couldn't look his son in the eye.

"It's okay, pop," said Aaron. "I forgive you, as well. For everything."

"How?" asked Karl. "I lied to you all your life. You don't know who you are, who your father is. How can you forgive me for that?"

"I know who I am—my name is Aaron Engel. If the man that sits before me is my father, then the secret that you've held for so long, the hell you've put yourself through, only makes me love you more. You are the man that raised me, and nothing that you've said diminishes the love that I've grown with all my life.

"If the other man, who died in the camp, is my father, then he is also forgiven, for I would not be here today if he had not given his life, sacrificed himself, for his family. Both of you are heroes. I know mom loved you, I know you made her very happy. Please, don't forget that. She would be very proud of you today."

Aaron paused when his father wept, fiercely, into his aged hands.

"Now, I understand," Aaron continued, "why you refused to sell the bakery a decade ago, when the recession hit and times were hard. I want you to know that I will keep it open, and I will raise my children to understand its importance, so that it will remain in our family even after I'm gone."

Agent Williams opened the door, followed by Agent Stein.

"Mister Engel," began Williams, "I just received a call from the Wiesenthal Center, not in New York City, but in Paris, from a very important person, fully corroborating your story. It seems that the person we spoke to before, in New York, was also in the dark about a lot of this. Turns out, that your sister, Sarah, is a retired employee with the Center, and had falsified documentation declaring the Nazi Karl Engel killed in World War Two, to protect you should anyone come looking for you. All of which I'm sure you knew, since you kept in touch with her, even minimally.

"That was her on the phone. Apparently, she had given explicit instructions that if anyone had ever contacted the Center asking about Karl Engel, she was to be telephoned immediately. Maybe, sir, enough time has passed that, whatever happened between you two fifty years ago, can finally be swept away. We are taking the liberty of flying her to Louisville, on our dime, for a family reunion."

Karl cried once more. "Thank you for bringing her here. I knew it was only a matter of time before she would be calling you, telling you everything I said to be true. Still, I needed to get all of this off my chest, anyway."

"I want you to know," continued Williams, "that you have my sincerest apologies and, as you stated when all of this started, you will not be charged with crimes against humanity—all charges are hereby dropped. The Bureau, itself, would also like to extend its sincere apologies for what you and your family have been put through today. While no one here understands what you have lived through, we know that it was extremely difficult for you to relive those darkest of memories. Is there anything that I can do for you?"

The Camp

"No, thank you. And, don't trouble yourself for today's events—if it took the FBI fifty years to track me down, then I did my job well." Karl smiled.

"Mister Engel," said Agent Stein, "I believe that I owe you the greatest apology. I did not know. My behavior, my language, has been terrible, and you have shown nothing but patience toward me. If you would like to file a complaint with--."

"That won't be necessary," Karl interrupted. "I accept your apology. The best thing you can do if you want to make it up to me, is to recognize that you need to learn two things from this experience. First, be very careful using the 'ignorance' defense. I heard that too often after the war. Ignorance is never an avenue that makes hatred, or plausible deniability, acceptable.

"The second thing is to have more control over your own emotions. If you allow yourself to be consumed by hatred for those who hate you, you will be no better than them."

Karl smiled and stood, patting Stein on the shoulder, using the young agent as a prop to help him stand.

"If I may," said Stein, "I'd like to walk you to your son's car."

"That would be fine."

"So, you really did just walk right out of camp?"

"Out of camp? Yes. Out of Europe? No."

"Well, I'd love to hear how you and your wife, and younger sister, escaped. I'm sure the journey couldn't have been easy. Klaus and Claudia never figured it out?"

"It was not easy, my young friend. But, I'm very tired now, and all that, including Klaus and Claudia, is a story for another day. Perhaps you can come by the house in a few days, and I'll do my best to remember as much as I can. I assume the FBI has my address."

Agent Stein laughed. "Yes, sir, we do. I have a day off this coming week, if you don't mind me coming over then."

"I look forward to it," said Karl.

The old man shuffled his feet down the hall, flanked by his son on one side, and his new friend on the other.

Acknowledgments

I want to thank my beta readers for all their helpful advice: Sally Smith, Kim Abell, Lynne Markie, and Marianne Graft. I also want to next thank my wife, Stephanie Hair, of Capture Me Photos, for the incredible cover.

Made in the USA
Lexington, KY
09 October 2014